"Do you know who I am?"

"Yes."

What else was she supposed to do?

"I need to make sure there's not more bleeding." She gingerly slid her fingers through his hair, searching for any injury that would make moving him dangerous. "You have a funny look on your face. Please tell me you can see okay?"

With the light off him, he had been watching her. His expression suggested that he thought her a figment of his imagination.

"Cain. Stop trying to scare me. Speak."

Just as she was about to hold up two fingers and ask him how many he saw, he framed her face within his hands and drew her down for a kiss…

Dear Reader,

Welcome to Almost, Montana, population...not many. Prospects...challenging. It was the home of Cain Paxton, before he was sent to prison for a crime he didn't commit, and it was the latest stopping point—the longest to date—for Merritt Miller, a young woman with a past that she was trying to forget.

The future looked uncertain for these two drifter-misfits who didn't seem to belong anywhere, or to anyone. Creating a family of two, and filling their lives with people they chose and weren't linked to by birth or law wasn't something they did consciously, but the evolution of it proved a lifesaver for both of them.

I suppose I was drawn to the idea of Merritt and Cain due to having been a lifelong observer and supporter of survivors, people who take life's blows, and refuse to be defeated. Showing that love waits, even for the loner and the lonely, was an especially satisfying experience.

I hope you enjoy Merritt's and Cain's journey. And, as always, thank you for being a reader.

With warmest wishes,

Helen R. Myers

First published in Great Britain 2012
by Mills & Boon, an imprint of Harlequin (UK) Limited,
Eton House, 18-24 Paradise Road, Richmond, Surrey TW9 1SR

© Helen R. Myers 2012

ISBN: 978 0 263 89425 7
ebook ISBN: 978 1 408 97838 2

23-0412

Harlequin (UK) policy is to use papers that are natural, renewable and recyclable products and made from wood grown in sustainable forests. The logging and manufacturing processes conform to the legal environmental regulations of the country of origin.

Printed and bound in Spain
by Blackprint CPI, Barcelona

Helen R. Myer is a collector of two- and four-legged strays, and lives deep in the Piney Woods of East Texas. She cites cello music and bonsai gardening as favorite relaxation pastimes, and still edits in her sleep—an accident, learned while writing her first book. A bestselling author of diverse themes and focus, she is a three-time RITA® Award nominee, winning for *Navarrone* in 1993.

Chapter One

"Lock up your women and check your ammunition supply, men. Cain Paxton is back in town!"

The sun had yet to crest the trees interspersed throughout Almost, Montana, but Merritt Miller had already heard variations of that warning at least four times since the first customer had shuffled into Alvie's café shortly after 6:00 a.m. After the second alert, Merritt had gone to ask Alvie Crisp herself about the matter, as the sturdy woman worked.

"Who's Cain Paxton?" Martha had asked.

Barely glancing up from her work, single-handedly preparing breakfast for a near capacity crowd, Alvie had replied, "Someone you better not give two seconds of thought to, Miller Moth." Pausing, the salt-and-pepper-haired woman wiped perspiration from her broad forehead with the back of her left hand. Outside, it might be struggling to stay above twenty-eight, but it was always somewhere between toasty and roasting in the kitchen. "Just another mother's heartbreak," Alvie continued, "another father's shame."

Merritt had ignored the nickname Alvie had given her on the first day she'd begun working here, now over two years ago. It was milder than some she'd been called in her twenty-seven years. She knew she was a drab specimen of womanhood compared to the pampered daughters and wives who sometimes dined here when reluctantly staying in town to shop if weather or time didn't allow them to get to Montana's larger cities like Bozeman or Billings on either side of them, or the state capital, Helena, to their north. Her petite, thin frame had never turned heads, nor had her pale face earned studied admiration. Her one good feature—her dark brown hair—had to be constantly tied back by an elastic band because there was plenty of it. In these last three years of her "emancipation," as she secretly dubbed it, she'd come to the conclusion that she was meant to sit alone on the grocery shelf of life. If her unspectacular looks weren't reason enough, her semi-lameness made it official.

"I was just wondering what the fuss was all about," Merritt said softly as she returned again to pick up the twin plates brimming with ham, eggs over easy, hash browns and biscuits with gravy for table three. The only Paxton she knew owned one of the biggest ranches in the area, and as far as she knew he was an aging widower and childless. "Usually all anyone wants to talk about is the price of beef, feed, cranky machinery or how your cooking has 'hit the spot.'"

Alvie grunted as she turned another batch of thick-sliced bacon. "Helps to be the only joint in town. After you deliver those plates and refresh everyone's coffee mugs, come on back here. I want to talk to you about the latest weather report I heard on the radio."

"Is the storm coming in early? From the looks of the skies, it sure seems like it will be a strong one." Merritt didn't know how the woman discerned anything with the thing turned so low. All she was hearing over the conversations flowing in from the dining room was static.

"That it is, and it's going to be worse than they thought. Now move, child."

Merritt went with a slight smile rather than hurt feelings. She was well used to Alvie's frank, no-nonsense approach to things and that was also reflected in her appearance. Her employer's clean-scrubbed face was as bare of makeup as her own. Alvie's hair was shorter, but still pulled back into a tight bun. As always in cold weather, she wore a white chef's apron over overalls and a man's plaid flannel shirt. Today's was mud-brown, like her hiking boots. No frills for the woman who had buried two husbands and a daughter; she said what she meant and meant what she said. But her heart was gold. Merritt could vouch for that. Alvie had been the one to give her a job and a place to stay when she'd first arrived here with barely enough money left in her wallet to pay for a night's stay in a cheap motel—if there'd been such a thing in Almost.

On the way up front, Merritt grabbed a full pot of the aromatic coffee from the machine's secondary hot plate, then delivered the two platters to ranchers who never paused in their intense conversation. They were regulars and knew that unlike the other waitress, feisty and flirty Nikki Franks, she didn't crave small talk with them, let alone anyone to flirt with. She topped off their mugs, then continued around her half of the café to see who else needed another dose of caffeine before braving the day's weather.

After returning to the kitchen, Merritt watched Alvie remove the bacon and add a slab of sirloin for one of Nikki's hungrier customers. Then she started on two orders of scrambled eggs. As she often did, Merritt picked up the ladle in the nearby bowl and stirred the pancake batter to keep it from settling.

"So how much snow do they expect?"

"Maybe a foot before you head home tonight. Twice that before we open in the morning."

Since Merritt had spent her whole life where snow was common, and this wasn't her first winter in Montana, she wasn't immediately intimidated. Besides, Thanksgiving was just around the corner. It might not say "winter" on the calendar, but frigid weather had definitely dipped below the forty-ninth parallel from Canada. "Okay. Guess I better arrange to come in earlier tomorrow." As a rule, she arrived minutes before the doors opened at six o'clock.

That earned her a critical look from Alvie. "I want you to be kind to your body and spend the night upstairs on my couch."

Alvie had many good qualities, but coddling didn't seem to be in her DNA any more than hugging was. Nevertheless, Merritt had been the recipient and witness of enough kindnesses by the two-time widow to know she had a soft side that appeared when she wanted it to. Apparently, this was one of those moments.

"You know I have to see to matters at the house. The barn cats will be craving some warm milk, especially tonight, and the stove needs tending to keep the pipes and Wanda and Willy's tank from freezing."

Wanda and Willy were her goldfish, the only pets she allowed herself to have, except for the stray cats that had been homesteading the barn on and off since it was built decades ago for Alvie's grandmother, who'd been a bride at the time. The house still belonged to Alvie, a one-bedroom wood-frame dwelling on several acres of land. It had stood empty for some time because it was more convenient at Alvie's age to live upstairs in the apartment over the café. Alvie had let Merritt stay there as part of her salary the minute she learned Merritt could bake.

"And what if Leroy can't get the truck started in the morning and come get you?"

It wouldn't be the first or last time, Merritt thought wryly. Alvie's live-in boyfriend handled the counter traffic at the café and seemed genuinely sweet on Alvie, but he was pretty useless as a mechanic or with most handyman chores. "Don't worry. I'll walk as I usually do."

With a sigh of exasperation, Alvie pointed at her with her stainless spatula. "You fighting blizzard-strength winds when there's not so much as a truck tread to follow to ease your way is an invitation for trouble, especially at that hour. Besides, you already spend more hours on your feet than any doctor would say is sensible. If you *went* to a doctor, which you won't."

Merritt prepared two more baskets of biscuits and bran muffins rather than wasting her breath. The walk was barely a mile, and doctors cost more money than she could afford. She already knew what she needed for her damaged hip from the one time she did need to get medical input, and she definitely couldn't afford that. Why go again?

"Walking has helped me build up my strength," she said when Alvie finally finished. "And when have I ever not pulled my weight around here?"

"You work harder than Nikki or Leroy combined," Alvie acknowledged. "That's another reason I need you to be reasonable."

She had dough rising at the cottage for this afternoon's baking, too. Merritt's mind was made up. She was going home. Thankfully, the cowbell on the café's door sounded and saved her having to further explain. After taking one of the baskets and accepting the omelet she'd been waiting on, Merritt headed up front again.

She grew aware of the changed atmosphere even before she rounded the lunch counter. Silence loomed throughout the large room. Then she noticed that almost everyone was staring at the newcomer standing just inside the entryway. He was an imposing figure as he fought the wind to pull the door closed behind his frame, big-boned with plenty of muscle to reinforce that. He succeeded with that wrestling match, then scanned the room with a combination of wariness and the same resentment some were radiating toward him. One look at his Native American coloring and stern features immediately had a number of diners shifting around to return to their meals. The rest took their time, but conversation remained a whisper of what it had been.

The stranger wasn't basketball-player statuesque, but he had to be at least six feet, which was intimidating to a woman who had to stretch to make five-three. There was something about the man's bearing that made Merritt think of the mountains she liked to look at from her kitchen window at the cottage as she washed dishes. His denim jacket was too light for this weather, and it and his jeans were a half size too small. No wonder Nikki was staring open-mouthed from the far corner of the room. Usually, the flame-haired Energizer Bunny pounced on any and every male who walked through the front door if they weren't regulars with an established preferred seating choice. She even dressed to entice; today she was wearing a skintight green sweater and jeans that left little to the imagination. But this man was no one to trifle with. Although she hadn't yet heard his name spoken, Merritt realized she had to be looking at Cain Paxton.

When his gaze fell on an open seat at the counter, the man sitting beside it shifted his hat onto it. Ashamed at one of Leroy's regulars, Merritt quickly set her customer's plate before him and went to correct the situation.

"Sit anywhere."

The breathless quality of her voice told her that she was as rattled as everyone else. When his dark gaze zeroed in on her, she wondered if that was what being hit with a Taser was like.

"It appears some of your customers object to that," he said.

Swallowing, she tore her gaze from his and glanced around in desperation, ultimately focusing on the table beyond the far end of the counter in the corner of the café. It rarely got used and would probably be a tight fit for him, yet she still found herself saying, "Will that do, sir?" She maneuvered to pluck a menu from the counter, then awkwardly shifted between tables to lead him to the corner.

"Perfect," he told her.

Not surprisingly, he chose the chair against the wall that would allow him to face the door, but he could only manage to get one leg under the table. The other he stretched beside it and half out into the aisle. His thigh was larger than both of hers combined—and she supposed so was his boot size.

Her throat dry, Merritt all but rasped, "Coffee? Juice?"

"Just coffee. Black."

"I'll be right back."

What happened next was ridiculous, since Merritt knew perfectly well where that long leg was; nevertheless, as she turned away, like a bird fooled by its reflection in glass, she managed to walk right into it and trip. With no chance to protect herself, she fully expected to hit the floor face-first. Then, to her amazement, a strong hand slowed her fall. A heartbeat later, another completely averted catastrophe.

"Sorry, sorry," she mumbled. Wholly mortified, as

soon as he eased his grip she hobbled away without daring a look back at him.

The semisecluded location of the table had protected her from most diners' view; however, Merritt felt the concerned inspection of those who had witnessed it, and her cheeks burned with embarrassment. She thought some were thinking, *Serves you right,* for not refusing him service. But Alvie hadn't given any such order. Second-in-command Leroy had kept his back to the room the whole time—although she could see him watching in the mirrored backsplash. So what choice had she had but to do her job? She had no reason to treat him the way everyone else was.

Willing herself to calm down, she put the mug and coffeepot on a tray, along with a napkin, silverware and a basket of the muffins and biscuits, and carried it back, accepting that she couldn't get a filled mug to his table without sloshing half of it onto the floor. Upon reaching his table, she set the potbellied ceramic before him and poured with an inane amount of care.

"You hurt yourself," Cain said, observing her and not the painstaking service.

"No, I'm fine," she said reluctantly as he made the observation.

"You're limping."

"That's old news," she said, frowning as she set the pot on the tray and dug her pad out of her apron pocket. "Do you need another minute to decide on what you'd like?" It didn't look like he'd touched the menu.

"Steak...bacon...hash browns...three eggs, sunnyside up, biscuits and gravy...and a side order of pancakes."

It would take her most of a week to eat all that, but Merritt wrote it all down, then set the basket in the middle of the table. "These are warm muffins and biscuits. I'll bring you a bowl of gravy right away so you can nibble while you wait on the rest."

She did her best to walk quickly and normally, fully aware that he would be watching her, but that was a joke. She'd been struggling even when she'd stepped off that Greyhound bus for the last time in three years.

Once she got to the kitchen, she clipped the ticket on the carousel before the older woman's face. "He's here."

Alvie looked at the ticket and her unpainted, wrinkled mouth twisted into something closer to acceptance than pleasure or amusement. "Yeah, he is. Cain always did like his breakfasts."

"Has he been away long?"

"Served most of a three-year sentence."

"He's been in prison?"

"Could have been worse. Some say he intended to kill the guy who was beaten."

Merritt had noted his hands just as she had the rest of him. She had to fight a shudder at the idea of being on the receiving end of their wrath. "But if he didn't actually do that, why did he get convicted?"

"Because the victim filed charges. Listen, Miller Moth, there was a hit-and-run. The guy killed was Cain's uncle. Someone figured, who would worry about one less drunk Indian? Cain got enough information to conclude who did it and he went after him. The problem was the driver was also the foreman at the Paxton Ranch."

"How terrible." But Merritt was confused. "Wait a minute—Cain's Native American and his name is Paxton, too?"

"Yeah," Alvie said with a heavy dose of sarcasm. "Small world, isn't it? Cain's father was Sanford Paxton's only son. Cain's mother was full-blooded Sioux. But as far as Sanford was concerned, that salad dressing never got concocted, understood? Now go take care of the rest of your customers before they change their minds about tipping you."

"Yes, ma'am."

First, though, she brought Cain the promised gravy and a saucer to pour it on the biscuits. Then she refilled coffee cups again, ending with his.

"Need another basket?" she asked when she realized he'd devoured everything.

"That's tempting, but I'll wait for the rest of my meal. Alvie's stuff is better than I remembered."

"I appreciate that. I do the baking now."

At the end of the counter, she signaled Leroy to hand over a plastic tub to save her having to walk around. Once he did that, she pocketed her tips and cleared off two emptied tables. She and Nikki bussed their own tables and helped load the washer if Leroy was backed up at the counter. The only good thing about the extra work was that they didn't have to split their tips with busboys.

By the time she finished, Alvie was calling, "Order, Merritt!"

She balanced the basin on her good hip and tried to ignore the ache in her right one. Her injury provided its own weather report. She would need an extra-strength pain reliever to get any sleep tonight.

After setting the basin on the long stainless steel counter, Merritt picked up the long platter that they usually used for dinners, now heaping with what Cain Paxton had ordered, plus the cake plate stacked with three pancakes. Once again picking up the coffeepot, she delivered Cain Paxton's breakfast and refilled his mug.

"If there's nothing else, I'll be back to top off your coffee in a few minutes."

"That'll be fine."

Since he didn't bother looking up from the meal that he was already in the process of devouring, she placed his ticket on the corner of the table and returned to her other customers. She didn't mind his reticence. She had to force herself to make polite conversation. Half the people who came in treated her as though she was part of the fixtures. Nikki was the one who got—and frankly invited—attention. *She can have it,* Merritt mused, thinking of some of their less palatable clientele.

The crowd started thinning out shortly after that. Almost everyone cast speculative looks toward Cain on their way out. Merritt wondered how many of them knew about his past. Probably everyone. Revenge was never right or wise, but it sounded like Cain had been pushed to an impossible limit, given his added parentage dilemma. Merritt supposed people were thinking a convict was a convict and the taint was eternal.

Before Merritt could bring the coffeepot back to the corner table, Cain rose and carried his plates and mug to the end of the lunch counter. Startled, Merritt rushed forward to take them from him.

"That's my job," she told him.

"You look like you could use the break."

He spoke matter-of-factly and his gaze barely brushed over her, making her feel less significant than she already did in her discount-store, beige pullover and jeans. "I'm fine," she said with a touch too much pride. "I work the dinner shift, too. I can do my job."

"Excuse me for trying to help." He slid a twenty-dollar bill across the counter. "Tell Alvie she hasn't lost her touch."

As he headed for the door, Merritt recovered enough to protest, "Your change, sir."

"Keep it," he said without looking back.

Merritt stared, stuck between the embarrassment of knowing that he'd overtipped her out of pity and confusion over why someone fresh out of prison would be so generous when he could ill afford to be?

Leroy plucked the ticket and twenty from her and made change. Of medium height and sinewy build, his steel-gray hair matched his full mustache and beard and framed a sardonic face with shrewd eyes and a down-turned mouth. Unlike her, he had an opinion on everything and didn't wait to be asked for it.

"You be careful, honey," he said, handing her the tip money.

"Me? What did I do?"

"You got his attention. That's enough."

That was the silliest thing he'd said in a good while. "He's blaming himself for my limp when I clumsily tripped over his leg. I tried to explain."

"Didn't see that. But what I do know is that you're female, and he tipped you nice. Cain's always been a magnet to women. Just one of nature's mysteries. Maybe Alvie told you that he's been locked up for a good while, too?"

"But he's hardly blind," Nikki said, bringing her own ticket and cash for him to handle. She cast Merritt a saccharine, deal-with-it smile.

Ignoring her, Merritt untied her apron and went in back, thinking about Cain's parentage. For a small town like Almost with a population of barely five thousand, that was a good deal of scandal and intrigue. The outcome seemed unjust, too.

Alvie was beginning to prep for the lunch crowd. The restaurant business remained a fascination to Merritt, but there was no denying that it was a physically demanding way to make a living.

"If you don't mind, I'm heading to the house to get things ready for the weather," she told her boss.

"Take the truck. I heard most of what you said to Leroy just now."

"I *tripped*—I didn't fall. I'm fine." Merritt appreciated Alvie's concern, but there was such a thing as overkill. "And remember that I don't have a license." She'd never bothered transferring her New Jersey license because she hadn't known how long she would be staying. She continued to resist because she could walk to wherever she needed to go, or catch a ride with Alvie or Leroy, which let her save money, and now her old New Jersey license had expired.

"No one is going to stop you—unless you run over the chief of police himself. They're sure not going to bother you in deteriorated weather conditions—or give you a ticket for coming to work. They know where you belong." Alvie shook her head. "I don't see why after all this time you won't get a driver's license."

Having a license meant she could be traced. But Merritt wasn't going to share that bit of information unless she was forced to hit the road again. With a negligent shrug, she said, "I'll see you by four-thirty, okay?"

"Might be a slow night if things get bad really fast. If you had a phone, I could tell you to save yourself the trip and stay home."

People living sparely could do without such luxuries as a phone, especially someone not anticipating a call from anyone any more than she desired one. Giving up on arguing with the woman she owed her job and home to, Merritt waved and detoured to the back room where she changed from sneakers into boots, slipped on her jacket and retrieved her big insulated tote that she'd carried her baked goods in.

Two other waitresses with school-age children handled the lunch crowd. Leroy took over the grill, while Alvie went upstairs to rest her feet or run errands. Then Alvie returned while Leroy took off, since the dinner crowd usually left the counter empty enough for Merritt and Nikki to manage on their own.

Almost—its name origins in dispute forever—began perhaps by survivors of an Indian attack, *almost* making it through the Rockies on their way to Idaho, then Washington. Another claim was that a wagon train had *almost* been wiped out by a deadly winter and disease. However it was christened, the town had remained the same size building-wise as it was at its peak prior to World War II. It was a two-traffic-light community, six blocks in all, which included one bank, two pharmacies, five churches and a school that still housed kindergarten through grade twelve. The only difference was that half the stores on back streets were vacant now. A few were collapsing from neglect, having been tied up in estate disagreements. There was a good deal of talk about what to do to sustain what economic stability there was and encourage tourism from the interstate only two miles south. Merritt felt she had no right to get involved with any of that, but hoped things worked out for the residents, particularly the business-people.

Living in Alvie's house was a rent-free agreement since she provided all of the baked goods for the eatery. Merritt paid half of the electric bill, which remained in Alvie's name, so funds were just taken out of her pay. She was thinking about that bill which she expected to arrive today or tomorrow, as she started around the bend that hid the cabin from downtown's view. That compromised view made it susceptible to vandalism, which was another reason why Alvie was eager to have it lived in.

The wood-frame cottage with the peeling gray paint consisted of a combination kitchen-dining area and a living room with just enough room for the sofa and chair in it, as well as the wood-burning stove. The kitchen stove was propane, but Merritt had gotten the hang of it quickly enough. The bathroom was off the back door, by the washroom, and the bedroom was on the other side of the dining area. The full-size bed was perfect for someone of her size, but she couldn't imagine a couple even Alvie and Leroy's size trying to sleep comfortably on there for long.

With no central air or heat, the wood-burning stove required careful tending in cold weather. While Alvie kept the place in a good supply of wood, it had taken Merritt most of her first winter in Montana to learn how to finesse its operation.

Merritt lifted her face to the sky and felt the first flurries sting her nose and cheeks. Not only did the damp cold seep through her bark-brown, thrift-shop jacket and thin frame, every step cost her extra energy due to the pain now spreading across her back because of the strain on her muscles. She would need to lie down for a few minutes with a hot compress once she reached the cabin, and that would only make her busier the rest of the day if she was to get her baking done in time. Thank goodness she'd already completed her weekly washing and cleaning. She definitely wouldn't have to worry about anyone coming to visit her and taking up her time because, while she was polite to anyone who spoke to her, she had no friends to spend her off-hours with. That was the price she paid to ensure she could continue to live here safely. From her perspective it was an acceptable cost.

But as she rounded the curve that gave her the first view of the cottage, she immediately saw something that triggered concern. There was a black truck parked on the street in front of the property. Had someone experienced engine trouble or a flat? No one had passed her as she'd walked, and she didn't recognized the old, paint-worn pickup. Yet the vehicle was facing away from her, suggesting that's what must have happened.

What if someone was casing the place? If they had a good reason to be there, they would have pulled into the driveway, wouldn't they? And yet she didn't see anyone, just the truck. Could they already have broken in?

Running wasn't an option unless she wanted to end up flat on her face for sure this time, but Merritt increased her pace, which had her breathless and her face strained with pain by the time she got to the driveway. There she saw a man climb the far steps of the porch and return to the front window where, with his hands framing his eyes, he tried to look inside the front window.

"Hey! What do you think you're doing?" she shouted.

He turned immediately and Merritt's breath caught in her throat. It was Cain Paxton! In a heartbeat, her indignation vanished, only to be replaced by anxiety. She self-consciously limped up the short drive, and was panting when she reached the base of the porch stairs.

"How did you know where I live?" she demanded as wind whipped at her jacket and hair.

He shoved his hands deep into the denim jacket pockets and tucked his neck into his shoulders. His black hair, though not overly long, whipped wildly around his face. "I didn't. I stopped thinking the cabin might still be empty. Thought I'd ask Alvie how much she wanted for rent."

"It's taken—by me."

He gave her a slower head-to-toe inspection than he

had before, and then looked over her shoulder. "Heck-uva day to be without your car."

"I don't have one."

That earned her a frown that made him appear tougher and angrier. Add that to the wind and cold's effect on his hair and square-jawed face, and she thought it gave him an otherworldly air—an unholy one. How on earth could Leroy think she could be taken by such a force of nature, even without knowing her past?

"You walked the whole way?" he asked, his tone as scornful as his expression. "What kind of glutton for punishment are you?"

That was just what she needed at this point, a warrior god with a vegetable for a brain. "A poor one," she snapped back.

Cain fell silent again, but he continued to study her. Merritt wanted badly to get inside and out of the wind, but she wasn't budging while he was blocking her way.

"How long have you been in Almost?" he finally asked. "Not long enough to learn that it's dangerous to walk outside town by yourself."

"Sorry to disappoint you, but I've been doing just fine. From what I've been told, I guess I arrived not long after you left."

The right corner of his hard mouth twitched and a timeless sensuality lit in his black eyes. "So you've been asking about me?"

"What I asked was why some of our regulars are so uptight over your return. Alvie gave me a quick recap.'"

Cain snorted. "No wonder you looked like a lamb ready to bolt when you saw me walk in. Relax. Having just arrived, I'm not about to get myself a one-way ticket back into prison. Besides," he added with another cursory glance over her shivering body, "there's not enough to you to make an appetizer for someone with my tastes."

"Rape isn't about desire," she said without thinking. "It's about anger and control."

"Is that so?"

Merritt all but lost the rest of her courage under his narrow-eyed stare. She felt as though he was doing more than stripping her; he was peeling the layers of her skin. Seeking what, she didn't know. But she had to lower her gaze in self-defense, afraid that her cold shivers would turn into an outright shudder. Belatedly, she thought about how to casually dig for the pepper spray buried in the large tote beside her wallet.

When she didn't come back at him with any cheeky answer, he asked almost kindly, "What's your name? It's only fair," he added when she shot him a doubtful glance. "You know mine."

"Merritt Miller."

"And I thought I got stuck with a whopper. Was your daddy hoping for a son?"

"No, I was named after my paternal grandmother. I'm told she was very pretty and had a sunny disposition, and they called her Merri. Me, they called Merritt." The wind was bringing tears to her eyes and she blinked them away, hoping he didn't see them and misunderstand. "Now that we have that out of the way, would you mind going on about your business? I have to get the stove ashes emptied and a new fire going. You may not have heard that there's a storm coming, and I'm working the dinner shift. It'll take half the night to warm that cabin if I don't keep a good bed of coals in that thing." As soon as she spoke, she wanted to clap her hand over her mouth. Why tell him the house would be empty later?

However, Cain didn't focus on that. He asked instead, "You mean you're walking back to town? What the hell is wrong with those people? Why doesn't Leroy or someone pick you up?"

"Because they're busy. Besides, I need to walk whether I want to or not. It's therapy."

"Therapy." Once again his gaze swept downward. "You're healing from an operation?"

"No."

"So you should have an operation, but you won't, and to keep your hip from totally freezing up you have to keep moving?"

"Something like that."

"Bet that feels like crap. What happened?"

For a seemingly quiet man, he'd suddenly turned into a blabbermouth. "I fell."

"Uh-huh. Probably from clumsiness again, like this morning?"

Merritt knew what he was trying to do; however, the words stung anyway. "That's right," she replied, stiffly.

Cain glanced at the dwindling pile of firewood on the porch. "I'll get the stove going for you, but you need more wood than what's left on your rack."

"There's more in back. I just haven't brought it up yet."

"I'll do that, too."

Dear heavens, was he looking for work? "Mr.

Paxton, I meant what I said about being poor. I get by with what I make at the café, but that's about it."

"Did I ask you for a job?"

"No."

Maybe it was her honest reply and expression that made him relax and shrug. "You led me to the best table in the café for someone in my situation. You didn't treat me like poison, or worse yet, dirt, as some have. Can't that be reason enough?"

She'd only done her job, and she wasn't one to buy into gossip. As far as she was concerned, he'd needed to be seated before he cost Alvie business. As a new, stronger blast of wind cut through her jacket, she couldn't quite stifle a groan. She wanted a hot mug of tea—and a painkiller—more than she wanted to argue semantics or social prejudice with this man. Besides, if he was a threat to her, he could easily have already made his move.

With a curt nod, she climbed the stairs in the only way she could—left leg leading, right leg slower to follow. When she made it to the porch, she unlocked the door.

The cabin was cooling, but not yet uncomfortable. Merritt went immediately to the fish tank and tapped on the glass. "I'm back. It'll be better in a few minutes."

The door closed with a thud. "You're talking to fish?"

Merritt didn't bother looking over her shoulder; she could tell by the tone of Cain's voice that he thought her ridiculous. "I work too many hours to have a dog or cat." She wasn't going to admit there were cats in the barn. They were wild—or at least independent—and she was a bit scared of them.

"How smart is it to torture yourself for a couple of overpriced goldfish?"

"They know their names—Wanda and Willy." She finally made herself glance back at him and got a blank stare in return. "From the movies *A Fish Called Wanda* and *Free Willy?*"

With a brief shake of his head, Cain crossed to the stove and flipped open the damper in the flue. That's when his expression changed. He'd undoubtedly noticed what she'd been fretting about since lighting her first fire this season.

"It feels like the damper is about shot. It's hanging on one side. By chance do you have another?"

"Do you mean this?" Merritt went to the brick wall behind the stove and picked up the round piece of metal that had been on the ledge for as long as she'd been a resident. Early on, Alvie had told her it would need to be changed one day when the old one wore out. "I'd hoped it would last until spring when I could let the stove cool enough to work in there."

"You thought you could do this yourself? First of all, your arms are too short to reach in and up that high. Second, how did you expect to hold it in place and still stand outside and slip in the rod to secure it?"

"I guess I didn't think," she admitted.

He grunted his agreement and opened the door on the stove to gauge what he was dealing with. A moment later, he slipped off his jacket and tugged his T-shirt over his head.

"What are you *doing?*" Merritt gasped.

"These are the only clothes I own at the moment. I'd like to avoid ruining them."

The last man she'd seen in this state of undress had been her stepbrother, Dennis, whose skin was as pale as a corpse with a beer belly that hung so far over his jeans he resembled cupcake batter overflowing a pan. In comparison, there wasn't an ounce of flesh on Cain Paxton's bronze body that wasn't hard muscle.

"But you'll burn yourself."

Testing the side of the stove with his hand, Cain shrugged. "It's cooled down quite a bit. It shouldn't be too bad. I'll need you to help, though." He pulled the stem from the outside of the flue and the subsequent rattle and thud was indication enough that the old damper fell into the remaining few coals. "See this?" He showed her the steel pin with its twisted end designed for control by hand of the level of airflow. "When I stick the new damper up into the stack, you watch through that hole. When these slots are aligned to the opening, you stick this pin back through. You have to slip it all the way and make it come out the other side of the stack. Understood?"

"Is that even possible?" The slots weren't half the width of her pinky nail—and she'd heard too often than she had the hands of a preteen.

"It better be, or you'll freeze tonight as all of the heat rushes up and out of here through the stack." After opening the stove door, he nodded. "The buildup of ashes over the remaining coals will help suppress the heat," he said, lowering himself to his knees. "I'll leave them until I'm done."

Merritt didn't think he would get so much as his

head and a shoulder into the opening, but he managed. Nevertheless, it took several tries to get the damper replaced, partly because Merritt's hands were shaking from nervousness, partly because Cain had difficulty maintaining the correct position. But—after several muffled curses from him—suddenly the pin slid all the way through and out the opposite hole.

"Thank God," she whispered, almost weak with relief.

"As soon as I clean up, I'll get rid of those ashes and get you that wood," Cain said, trying not to touch his jeans as he rose to his feet.

Merritt saw how filthy he had indeed gotten on her behalf. "Please, the bathroom is to the left just before you go out the back door." She pointed through the kitchen. "Help yourself to soap and towels. Whatever you need. I really am grateful for your help, Mr. Paxton."

"The name is Cain. The only Mr. Paxton in these parts wouldn't take kindly to hearing you using his name in reference to me." Cain grimaced at his hands and the soot smeared over his arms and chest. "Do you have a couple of old rags? I don't want to ruin any frilly lady things. This creosote won't wash out easily."

As she wiped at a miniscule streak of soot on her hands, Merritt felt another blush threaten. "I don't own any frilly things. You use what you need to, and I'll put on a kettle for tea. You'll welcome that after being out in the wind again."

Chapter Two

As he headed for the bathroom, Cain's mood soured anew. He didn't want any tea, he wanted a beer...or better yet something stronger. But he doubted Miss Merritt Miller had ever tasted anything more potent than Communion grape juice, let alone allowed anything alcoholic in her house. That was yet another reason to get out of here, he thought, shutting the door behind himself.

It was ironic that he'd arrived in town early this morning with a deep-seated fire in his belly for justice; however, he'd barely begun digesting breakfast, and this scrawny, ghost-pale woman had succeeded in resurrecting the last two or three ounces of human compassion left in him and thrown him off his plan. He'd had no choice but to help her; there was no way she could have managed to repair the stove herself. Hell, he thought, gingerly checking the spots on his inner right arm and abdomen, he'd gotten burned himself a couple of times on the still-hot metal.

No telling what all needed attention around the place, he mused as he turned on the hot water tap and started soaping his hands. He remembered the house being old when he was a kid. Alvie and her first, then second, husband were living there then. And a baby. To the best of his recollection, the child had died in infancy—some influenza that had wreaked havoc on the area.

The Miller girl was keeping things spotless, he would give her that. As he noted the neatly folded, dark blue towel on the rack, which would do nicely for drying off, he figured she would get all puffed if she knew he was thinking of her as a girl—she was probably in her mid-twenties. But she didn't need him thinking of her as a woman. Having been deprived of female company for over three years—counting the months he'd gone crazy sitting in the county jail while his worthless public defender was bulldozed by Paxton money and influence—his fingers itched to bury themselves in Merritt Miller's lush brown hair. She wore it in a loose braid down her back, and not once did it sweep saucily across her cute butt. She was that quiet and steady of a mover. Everything moderated and even, despite the hip—maybe because of it.

Her scent was here, which made sense—it was the soap. Simple, clean. On her body it became feminine and delicate. Surrounded by it again, he breathed in deeply and almost groaned with pleasure. To regain his equilibrium, he leaned into the sink and scrubbed his face and hair. The amount of work it took reminded him that he needed a haircut. Badly.

He ended up having to use the hand towel as a wash-rag to get the soot off. By the time he was done, the burn on his belly and arm were seeping, so he checked the medicine cabinet for antibiotic ointment. He found it and a gauze pad for the worst one on his abdomen. He also found a package of throwaway razors. He'd inherited the Native American sparseness of body hair, but there was enough to get his attention, so he reached for one of the razors, too.

While there wasn't much room to maneuver in the small confines, Cain took a small pleasure in the privacy of the closed door. That's the one thing he had been most offended and affected by in prison. He was tempted to strip and step into the tub under the hot shower spray, but the little waitress didn't deserve to be thrown into another tailspin. He did, however, let himself imagine her behind that clear plastic shower curtain, naked and sleek from the water sluicing down her body. Her head would be tilted way back, her wet hair cupping her sweet bottom the way he wanted to.

What is her story? he wondered as he hung the soaked towels over the shower rod. While hardly beautiful by today's commercial standards, she had a child's flawless skin and pleasant enough, though not remarkable, features. Her serious eyes were a shade lighter than her mahogany hair. When she wasn't studying him like a dubious owl, there had been a sadness in their depths, and secrets. Those eyes would probably make heads turn if she used a little makeup, as would her mouth. It was small, but formed like a bud. Hell, he thought, if she just licked them moist, she could make a man lose his train of thought. If she would lick him—

A spasm in his groin reminded him that he'd been successful in the weight room and needed to look into getting a size larger jeans. He hissed as he adjusted his clothing, then slid on his T-shirt.

Get the damned wood for her and get out of here.

Yes, he had to go. Word would spread quickly that he was back, and he needed to move on to the reservation and see his grandmother. With the storm about to make driving difficult, he hoped she would put him up for a night or two until he figured out if it would be possible to get a job in the area, or if old prejudices would force him to move on. No doubt his grandmother could use a hand around the place, too.

He raked his hands through his wet hair and wished he'd taken the time for a haircut. No wonder Merritt, the little ferret, was spooked by him, he thought as he checked his reflection one last time before emerging from the bathroom. Better, he thought, but with his chin-length hair, he looked like one of his wilder ancestors.

Merritt was taking the tea bags out of the mugs and adding honey and lemon as he reached her. "I appreciate the hospitality," he said. "I didn't know where you wanted the towels, so I spread everything on the shower curtain rod."

"That's fine. And you can call me by my name. It's Merritt," she said as though guessing he hadn't paid attention before.

"I remember."

"I'll tell Alvie how kind you were." She pushed the mug across the counter toward him.

Noting her hands were trembling slightly, he murmured his thanks. "You might want to rethink that idea. She's always been decent to me, but she might not like the idea of me being anywhere near you—or being allowed into her house."

Merritt glanced up at him from beneath fine but surprisingly long lashes. "She's the one who told me about your uncle and the price you paid for trying to get justice for him. I'm sorry."

"Me, too—since I didn't succeed."

"Excuse me?"

Certain that Alvie had shared the official Paxton spin on things, he was determined to at least get his side told to someone other than people who would see the truth was buried. "My uncle lived long enough to give me a description of the vehicle and a partial license plate number. That told me the truck belonged to my father's ranch, and the driver turned out to be the ranch foreman, Dane Jones. I tracked him down determined to haul his worthless butt to the sheriff's office, only to find out someone beat me to him. Someone had knocked him senseless. And when the deputies arrived right on my heels, Jones let me take the fall for what happened to him."

"That's terrible. Couldn't your father intervene?"

"He died before I was born," Cain replied grimly.

"What about his father, your grandfather?"

When Cain sent her a "we're done talking" look, Merritt grew flustered. "Surely the authorities could see that your hands weren't bruised and that you hadn't been in a fight?"

"It's a long story." He shouldn't have said as much as he did, but he'd wanted her to understand what it meant to sympathize with a half-breed who was considered an outcast even by his own flesh and blood. The more she kept her distance, the better off things would be for both of them. Ignoring the tea, Cain went into the living room where he slid into his jacket and reached for the galvanized steel bucket behind the stove, then the shovel on the implement stand.

"I take it that your mother has passed, too?" Merritt asked from the wide kitchen entryway.

"I came into the world and she went out."

"Dear God. I'm sorry. Again."

"Ancient history. Look," he said, growing increasingly uncomfortable, "let me just get this stove cleaned out, and I'll get your wood. There are things I need to do."

"Of course. I can manage on my own now. Please don't make yourself late for my sake."

Embarrassment turned her cheeks the color of raspberries, which in turn made Cain feel like a creep. "I don't mean to insult you," he said with a patience he didn't feel. Why was he treating this little pest with kid gloves? He didn't care about anyone or anything anymore. At least that's what he'd told himself six thousand times while behind bars. "I just— I know you feel uneasy around me. For the record, that goes both ways."

Her expression made him think that he'd suddenly begun speaking in a different language.

"What am I doing that makes you uncomfortable?

There weren't enough words to answer her question, but she made him feel decades older than his thirty-three years. Concluding that it was best to leave Merritt with her naive perspective on small town law and order intact, Cain set into the task of filling the bucket with ashes, which he carried out back beyond the barn. It took two more trips before he was ready to start adding kindling to the remaining coals and get another fire going.

When he was satisfied that the fire would keep burning, he headed outside without further comment and started loading the rack onto the porch. It was snowing steadily now, and the intensifying wind started to carry the flakes horizontally.

At some point the mug of hot tea mysteriously showed up on one of the half-moon slices of hardwood, and he paused to take a few swallows, grateful for the relief against the cold. This kind of work in this kind of weather required a hat and gloves, neither of which he possessed yet. She knew—and wouldn't let him pretend it didn't matter.

Several trips later, he had enough wood to last her a few days. As he looked for a spot to set the empty mug so that he could avoid going inside again, the door opened. She'd wrapped herself in a shawl over her apron and turned away as occasional snowflakes slapped at her.

"I'll take that," she said softly. Her gaze only grazed him.

"I appreciate the gesture." He handed it over, careful not to make contact. Those damned hands were trembling again—or hadn't stopped. "I'll be on my way now."

"Be safe."

He didn't know if that was possible. He did believe getting away from here would improve his chances greatly. Nevertheless, when she retreated back into the house and closed the door, he felt—guilty? Something he couldn't describe, but he resented the feeling.

He turned up the collar of his jeans jacket, and his long-legged stride took him off the porch, skipping the stairs. Then he jogged to his truck, slipping several times, his cowboy boots slick on the wet snow.

Once in the truck, he glanced back at the cottage. If nothing had changed while he'd been gone, it was the only residence for another mile or so. In this weather the place looked more isolated than ever. But that wasn't his problem, he reminded himself.

He turned the key and had to floor the gas pedal before the old truck coughed and the engine reluctantly started. "Man, are you going to be a money pit," he muttered. Unfortunately, it was all that he could afford with the money he had.

As he drove toward the reservation, he forced himself to think forward and prepare for the reunion. He'd had no letters from home in the years that he'd been locked away. Except for his grandmother, there was no other immediate family, and Gran had never learned to write. Was she even alive? He tried to recall how old she would be, but couldn't. His mother had had two sisters besides the brother who'd been run over. The last he knew of either of them, one had moved to Nevada and the other to Wyoming. He needed to prepare for the possibility that there was no reason to stay in Almost.

With the extra-strength pain pill taking effect, Merritt was able to push back the blanket she'd been lying under and ease off the bed. It still depressed her that she moved like someone twice her age when she first got up after a nap, and especially after a full night's rest, but the house had warmed nicely. After one more mug of hot tea, she would be at full speed again—or as good as someone in her condition could be.

She hadn't meant to lie down, but the upheaval with Cain Paxton's arrival in town, added to the weather's effect on her body, had left her with little choice. Not if she intended to last through the dinner shift. Once in the kitchen, she turned on the oven before inspecting the several loaves of dough she'd reworked a last time and covered with clean damp dish towels before lying down. They would produce beautiful honey-cracked wheat bread and finish baking just in time for her to carry back to town.

Once she got them in the oven, she started on the cheese sticks that Alvie liked to serve with soups and salads. The corn bread would be next. She supplemented her income by baking for Alvie, as well as taking special cake and pie orders for birthdays, anniversaries and holidays. She'd been doing that since school, having learned early in life that she had to rely on her own income if she wanted to survive. Whatever money her mother had earned—when she'd been in any condition to work—went to booze, or was mooched or taken by whatever man was in her life. What had begun out of necessity had evolved into an enjoyable creative process. The labor proved an excellent tension outlet and therapy for a shy, frightened child, who needed healthy ways to escape a basket case home life.

As she mixed the shortening and flour, her mind inevitably drifted to Cain. Had he reached his grandmother? His truck looked to be twice as old as Leroy's, but at least it ran. For the moment.

She hoped he could make a new start. She had known her share of ex-cons in her twenty-seven years. Her mother had rarely hooked up with any other kind of man—until Stanley Wooten. Although Stanley was just lucky that he'd never been caught and locked away—like his son Dennis.

Shuddering, Merritt pushed them back into a dark hole in her mind and visually locked the door. No, she thought, Cain Paxton might look intimidating but, incredibly, he wasn't corrupted or evil yet. He'd shown her kindness and concern, and she'd seen shame and regret in his dark eyes. He wasn't lost. Yet.

The afternoon passed quickly and bit by bit product stacked on the counter, until Merritt knew she had to brave the intensifying storm outside and make the awful trek to town. As she packed her baked goods into the oversize thermal carrier, she hoped against hope that Leroy would show up at the road. But as she fed the wood-burning stove a last time, she knew the folly of such a wish. Leroy loved Alvie; however, that didn't mean that he was going to compromise his comfort by coming after her, even if she *was* key to making Alvie's business more successful. Especially not when he would first have to jump-start a battery that had needed replacing weeks ago.

Leaving on a kitchen light and a lamp near the aquarium for Wanda and Willy, she leaned down to the glass. "It should be an early night. Not to worry."

Outside, the stairs were already treacherous and covered with snow. Merritt tugged the shawl over her head farther down to protect her face and vision and made the descent with care, hugging the carrier like a baby. The wind was trying to turn it into a sail and lift her off the ground. Although it wasn't yet officially sunset, it was already growing dark. Locals and the errant vacationer would come to the café due to these awful conditions, which was the only reason she plodded on.

When she reached the road, she saw that her trail, even the truck's tire treads, were covered by new snow. Yes, she would make it to town, but could she make it home later? She hoped the few snowplows in the area were at least keeping downtown in navigable condition.

No more than a few dozen yards up the road, she heard the sound of a vehicle behind her. As she turned, she tried to identify the vehicle, hoping to get a lift the rest of the way—or, if it was a stranger, to have time to jump aside and not be hit. Surely the driver would see her bright red shawl?

The same beaten-up, black pickup that had been parked in front of her house earlier today slowed and stopped beside her. Cain leaned over and shoved the passenger door open for her.

"Get in," he yelled above the wind and motor.

Relieved beyond words, Merritt planted her thermal tote on the floorboard and then hoisted herself into the truck. It probably wasn't a graceful maneuver, but she wasn't auditioning for anything. "I'm grateful, Mr. Paxton—Cain. I didn't think you'd be back this way again. At least not today."

"Neither did I. I almost turned into your yard when I saw lights on, but then I spotted you up here. You are one stubborn woman."

"I like to think of myself as a responsible employee."

"Who takes foolish risks. You know you'd be less challenge to a wolf than a deer would be, even in this weather. I will admit you smell better than this lousy truck, though," he added. "I take it the baking was successful?"

"If you'll come inside for a few minutes when we reach the café, I'll get you a cup of coffee and a couple of my fresh rolls with herb butter as a thank-you for coming to my aid."

"I'll take you up on that offer."

His acceptance and the odd, weary note in his voice drew her attention. "So why are you heading back to town? Didn't you find your grandmother?"

"I did. She's dead."

Merritt didn't gasp, but all of her major organs reacted as though she had. "Oh, I am—" She paused realizing she'd been saying "sorry" incessantly to him today. "Sincere condolences," she managed, although the words sounded awkward to her ears. No telling how inane they must sound to him.

After several seconds he murmured, "Thanks."

"Was there someone to fill you in on what happened and when?" She hoped that he hadn't walked into an empty house and been forced to come to his own conclusions.

"Yeah, a cousin. It happened a year ago. Pneumonia. She wouldn't go to the clinic, not that it would have done any good at her age."

Merritt wasn't one to run to a doctor herself. She could only imagine how difficult the choice would be for someone who had no reason to trust another culture's medicine or didn't have the funds. "What will you do now?"

"Get you to work. Have another warm meal."

Sometimes it was a good thing to deal with only one detail at a time. She knew that from her own experience. But a million questions flooded her mind. Was there no one else to welcome him home? The cousin's parents? Siblings? Considering the weather, did no one have room to put him up for the night?

"I'll seat you in the same place if you like and make sure you get seconds of whatever you'd like."

"Don't get any ideas about turning me into your personal charity case."

And he called her stubborn? "Believe me, I can't afford to adopt you, and I have better things to do with my time than to beg you to accept my help so I can feel good about myself."

"Good."

As they rounded the curve, the lights of town came into view if not the buildings themselves. Merritt refused to speak again, having no desire to irritate what had to be a sore wound, or to be rebuked. She was curious as to where he would go after he ate—if he agreed to eat now. There was no motel in town, not even a bed-and-breakfast.

There were several cars already parked in front of the café. It would appear that a number of the shop owners had closed early, eager for a hot meal. None of them knew if there would be electricity at their homes so they could cook for themselves. A few were likely to spend the night in their own storage rooms on a cot.

With no parking place available, Cain simply stopped behind those parked to let her out. Merritt could tell he had changed his mind about coming in.

"Park in back," she told him. "I can let you in from the rear and you can eat in the pantry-storage room. That's where we take our breaks when it's slow."

Cain shook his head. He was focusing on a state police vehicle beside a sheriff's car. "I guess I'll pass. See you around."

Knowing it was a waste of her time to argue, Merritt scooped the tote into her arms. "The offer stands," she said before sliding gingerly to the ground. It took all of her body to slam the door shut; the wind was right in her face. She couldn't blame him for being reluctant to take on the law on his first day back, whether or not the people inside were the officers who'd arrested him. He was probably thinking of Nikki being there and ratting on how she was getting him a free meal in back.

Merritt thought about going around back herself, but it was dark and the footing could be treacherous depending on what Leroy had temporarily stacked in the alley. So she paused at the front door to stomp the excess snow off her boots and try to brush what she could from her shawl and jacket. By then Mr. Forrester, the independent insurance agent, came to hold the door open for her.

"Have to help the girl with the goods," he said, although he grimaced as his good deed earned him a face full of snow.

Others in the place turned and a few applauded. One pragmatic person hollered, "Shut the door! Draft!"

"I just served the last of your corn bread, sweetie," Nikki told her while taking an order at the start of her usual section. "I hope you have more."

Merritt responded with an enigmatic look. Nikki *hoped* she hadn't remembered or had run out of time. The young woman, who had changed into a lower-cut blouse for the evening shift, was as transparent as she was shallow. When she wasn't consumed with her own interests, she was undermining the other waitresses. The only time she noticed anyone else was if it was in her best interest to make a good impression in front of a customer, like now, or she was trying to figure out someone she saw as competition. While she was semi-living with Paxton ranch foreman Josh Bevans, Nikki made no bones about looking for a one-way ticket out of Almost. Preferably out of Montana. She honestly believed she was meant for bigger and better things.

"Any fried pies in there?" Sam Hughes asked. He owed the pharmacy at the other end of their block.

With an apologetic shake of her head, Merritt said, "Not tonight. I had some stove repair to deal with. Your favorite is chocolate, right? I'll get some made by tomorrow afternoon, okay?"

"You're a sweetheart, Merritt."

"And a Goody Two-shoes," Nikki murmured as she

brushed past her on her way to take an order ticket to the kitchen.

In her clunky boots, shawl and too-large jacket, Merritt felt frumpy bringing up the rear as the other waitress advertised herself by swaying her hips all but shrink-wrapped in a leather skirt. How Nikki managed to work the night in those open-toed, four-inch heels was nothing short of miraculous, but she didn't miss an opportunity to show off a pedicure any more than she did her other assets.

By the time Merritt set down her tote, and shed the shawl, jacket and boots, Nikki was back up front. Relieved, Merritt tied her sneakers, then went over to Alvie at the grill as she tied on her apron. "Looks like it will be busy despite the weather."

"You okay? How are the roads?"

"Already bad. Someone kindly gave me a ride."

"Good. Not a stranger?" Alvie asked, giving her a brief, stern look. "You watch for strangers even in these parts, Miller Moth. *Especially* in these parts."

To hide her guilty expression, Merritt turned to the tote to unpack. "You're going to love the cheese sticks. That new cheddar your supplier recommended works so well. I think I actually prefer them to the Parmesan."

"Knowing how much you love them, that's something. Bring me one when you finish—and tell Nikki to push the soup now that we have them. Did you have time to make the corn bread? Chili is moving tonight. No surprise there."

"Yeah, I heard Nikki served the last of them. I have two dozen muffins, which should get us through tonight easily enough."

"This weather makes people overindulge. If they keep inhaling the freebies the way they are, I'm going to have to go up on our prices. Everything okay at the house? You have enough wood? Did you leave the cabinet doors open under the sink before you left to try to keep the pipes from freezing?"

"Not to worry. It's all set."

"Child, you amaze me. I should have told Leroy to get his lazy backside over there earlier in the week to at least get the wood situation taken care of, but you know how he is. I'd be spending the rest of the week nursing *his* aches and pains instead of my own. And to add to the truck's battery problems, this afternoon he found a tire's gone flat."

Merritt might not own a vehicle, but she knew they required regular attention. A tire could go flat if the machine wasn't driven once in a while. Her bemusement turned to guilt as she realized that she'd let Alvie think she'd done everything herself. But as Cain had said, she'd only be making things difficult for both of them if she admitted he handled the difficult work and heavy lifting. So she finished unpacking and got out front as soon as she heard more diners arrive.

It was almost eight o'clock when Nikki's boyfriend drove his silver, diesel, three-quarter-ton pickup into a parking spot up front and tapped the horn lightly. Only three customers lingered over dessert at that point. Nikki waved to Josh and ran in back to tell Alvie she was headed off for the night.

"See you when I see you," Alvie drawled. She already had her area cleaned up and had begun her prep work for the morning.

It was general knowledge that maybe Nikki would be in and maybe she wouldn't. It depended on how deep the snowfall was by morning, and whether the female alley cat ever got to bed—or, rather, slept once she made it there.

In typical Nikki fashion, she stopped just outside the door and squealed at Josh, waving her hands in the air like a fictional maiden in distress. Merritt watched in quiet awe as Josh exited the warm cab to sweep her into his arms and carry her to the passenger side of the truck. No way was Nikki going to ruin her high heels, let alone plunge her bared toes in freezing snow. It would never cross Nikki's mind to bring a change of footwear—like boots—to work. Merritt had heard her say on more than one occasion that a man had to be trained from the start. If he wanted a show pony, he had to deserve one, and that cost attention as well as money.

Poor, foolish Josh, Merritt thought as the truck backed out of the slot. She caught a customer's signal and went to retrieve their ticket. By the time she brought them their change, Cain had entered.

He glanced around at the remaining diners, then took a counter seat at the far end of the kitchen. Merritt guessed he was still in no mood to be sociable and wanted to stay out of sight of the kitchen.

"I thought you'd given up on the idea of dinner," she told him as she brought a glass of water, silverware and a menu.

He ignored the menu and the question and asked, "What's the hottest thing Alvie has back there?"

"Chili or the soup. Today's is chicken-vegetable.

With noodles, not rice or potatoes," she added. Sometimes customers had a preference.

"I'll take the chili if you meant it about saving some bread for me?"

"You get corn bread with that, but I'll fix you a basket with a little bit of everything. You want to stick with water or are you up to a little more coffee? We also have hot tea or chocolate."

"Coffee."

Since he'd chosen the seat he had, she didn't prolong their conversation and resisted asking him where he'd been keeping himself for the last three hours. By now she'd convinced herself that he'd headed for the interstate and might be halfway to Helena, or maybe even en route to Idaho or Wyoming by now. Could he have parked in back and waited out the traffic in here? It was odd that he'd managed to miss Nikki and Josh.

Alvie wasn't pleased when Merritt arrived with an order ticket. But she relaxed when she learned it was for chili, which Merritt scooped into a bowl herself.

As Merritt moved to the container of grated cheddar, Alvie inspected the chili pot. "There's only a cup left in here." She reached for a cup. "You didn't eat two bites for dinner. Throw some cheese on this and swallow it quick before you head up front again."

Merritt demurred. "I really don't need beef in my system at this hour. Cain has a lumberjack's appetite, I'll give it to him."

The shrewd woman did a double take. "That's Cain out there? What's he doing hanging around town? I thought he went back to the reservation this morning."

Merritt prepared a basket of the breads for him and

tucked in two portions of the herbal butter. "It doesn't sound as though he's staying. He learned that his grandmother is dead. Did you know that?" Her boss usually was up to speed on all the news in town.

Alvie winced. "I did not. Didn't know her personally, either, but she seemed to be a steadying influence on him. What a rotten welcome home. Poor guy can't get a break."

Heartened by that generosity, Merritt saw the opportunity to come clean about today. "He stopped at the cottage when he left here. He was checking around when I got home. He said he was looking for a place to rent."

"More than likely hunting for something to hock. Did you have a problem chasing him off?"

"I started to until I saw who it was. Then I didn't see the need. I don't think he's a thief, Alvie. He just remembered the place as empty. It was an honest misunderstanding." Merritt decided she needed to know everything. "Alvie…the stove problem? He fixed the damper for me. He also restocked the wood inside and the stand on the porch. On his way back from the reservation, he gave me a lift."

Alvie's plump face went through several transitions before she puffed up her cheeks like a blowfish. "What do you mean letting a stranger in the house, young lady?"

"He's not a stranger," she whispered back, hoping the older woman would take the hint. "You and Leroy know him."

"But *you* don't. And none of us have a clue as to

what all has happened to him since he was put away. I declare, Merritt—"

"The stove is as good as new," Merritt reiterated. "If he hadn't been available, I'd be returning to a walk-in freezer this evening—and it's likely your customers might not have bread tomorrow."

Her calm tone and sound logic deflated her aggravated employer somewhat. "You have me there. Still, this isn't like you to accept so easily. Usually, you're as skittish as a filly around strangers, particularly men." Seeing Merritt's expression grow closed, she quickly added, "Okay, okay, so I reason through things out loud. I'm glad everything is back in order. Just be careful, will you? What you heard about him being something of a lady-killer isn't all exaggeration. Back before he got into serious trouble, you could count the female tongues hanging to the ground when he went through town. Even a married lady or two made fools of themselves inviting his attention. All that testosterone has probably only compounded being locked away in prison."

"He's been perfectly decent. Good grief," Merritt added, "you sound like you're lecturing Nikki. I'm no flirt."

"There's a first time for everything when it comes to the mysteries of chemistry. Look at me and Leroy. Better yet, don't. We aren't a pretty sight."

As Alvie laughed at her own humor, Merritt shook her head. "What you and Leroy share is uniquely yours. Don't make fun of that."

"I'm not, really," the older woman replied with a sigh. "I was more upset that you felt as though I was treating you like 'Miss Always In Season.' For the record, I don't waste my concern or breath on Nikki. I just live with the hope that she ups and takes off with some specimen before I have to fire her. She's exactly the kind to file for unemployment, and I would greatly resent having to pay half of that." Alvie nodded at the tray Merritt had prepared with the chili and bread-basket. "Dinner is on the house tonight. No doubt he'll get his back up, but tell him it's my appreciation for the help at the house."

Great, Merritt thought, picking up the tray. Now he'd get bent out of shape because she'd told Alvie every-thing.

To her surprise, however, Cain accepted the gesture. And, after he finished everything, including all of the breads, he agreed to a hot slice of apple pie, too. That's when Merritt understood that he was killing time in order to give her a lift home. Also to avoid the cold. That made her wonder where would he go afterward.

None of your business. Can't you see that even though he wants to stay in the warmth, he's trying to avoid eye contact so you won't get tempted to make too much small talk?

Determined not to make him see her as another emo-tionally starved woman, she did leave him alone and stayed busy refilling salt and pepper shakers then sugar containers throughout the place. Nikki never bothered with such trivial matters. After that she emptied the dishwasher and stacked the silverware up front, along with the glasses and, finally, the china.

They closed at nine, and Cain left only a minute before—their last customer. Merritt locked up after him and turned the sign in the window before finishing with clearing away his dishes. The last thing she did was pocket the tip that he'd left her. It wasn't as generous as earlier, but she would have been upset with him if it was. She knew he couldn't afford throwing money around, not with a truck in such dubious shape.

After turning off the lights, she returned to the kitchen. Alvie was removing her apron before turning off the lights and heading upstairs to Leroy. Now that it was quiet, Merritt could hear the TV playing. Once the kitchen lights were off, the sliding glass commercial cooler's fluorescent bulbs would provide the only overnight light in the place, along with the stairwell light leading to the upstairs apartment.

"Everything is shut tight up front, so I'll leave this way," Merritt said, gesturing to the back door. "Lock up after me?"

Alvie appealed to her again. "Please—spend the night. Or let me call over to the station and get whoever is on duty to drive you."

"No way." Merritt's stubborn Taurus personality helped her be resolute on the matter. It might be Officer Posner on duty, and he'd made her uncomfortable the one and only time she'd accepted a ride from him. Although he was married, Jerry Posner had asked too many personal questions and winked at her so often she'd begun wondering if he had a facial twitch. "I have my flashlight, and I'm going home to keep the cabin warm and start on tomorrow's baking. Tonight's bunch sure did chomp into our inventory. See you in the morning."

"Unless it's worse than they're saying it will be,"

Alvie amended. "Promise. If it's over knee-high, you be sensible and at least wait for a truck to clear the road. I'll serve toast if necessary and they'll eat it or else."

"And who'll wait on tables—especially if Nikki does lay out?"

Her boss rolled her eyes at their catch-22 dilemma. "God bless you, darlin'."

Smiling at Alvie's surrender as much as at her protectiveness, Merritt let herself out the back way and tugged the door shut behind her. The streetlights were on now and everything was illuminated extra due to the snow, which allowed her to avoid rodent surprises—the four- *and* two-legged varieties—and quickly emerge onto the side street sidewalk. There she was met by the wind again. It immediately pulled at the empty tote and her clothing, while the snow stung every inch of bare skin it could reach. Even so, Merritt was strangely calm. Somehow she knew she wouldn't have to walk far tonight.

Sure enough when she got to the corner, Cain's pickup rolled up beside her. Once again he leaned over to open the passenger door, but this time he gave no command for her to climb in.

As she had before, Merritt set her tote onto the floorboard and hoisted herself up into the seat. After slamming the door shut, she said, "I had a feeling you would do this."

"And I can't believe Alvie let you walk home in the dark." Cain turned on the directional light and turned left onto empty Main Street.

"I didn't give her any option. She wanted to call the police station and get whoever is on duty to drive me, but I wouldn't let her. I was afraid it would be Jerry Posner."

"Don't know that name. He must have hired on after I left."

Feeling blissfully cocooned in the warmth of the cab and enjoying the way the truck's headlights enhanced nature's temperament, Merritt allowed herself a franker reply than she ordinarily would have. "Your gain is our loss. He arrived about the time I did. I heard he transferred from another town. Probably to avoid having charges filed by some other poor soul he thought should be enamored of him."

Cain glanced her way. "What does that mean?"

"Nothing. I shouldn't have said anything."

After a pause, Cain said, "If Alvie doesn't know about how you feel, or if something happened, tell her. And if need be, you can talk to Matt Robbins. My experience with the law aside, the chief is okay."

That was her hunch, too, but Merritt's preference was to avoid any contact with a law official if possible. "All I want is to be left alone and do my job. Besides, causing him to be on the chief's radar would earn me Posner's resentment. No, thank you."

Cain let that be the end of the subject and, in another minute, pulled into her driveway. The maneuver required some acceleration and the rear end of the truck swung back and forth before steadying again.

"You could have let me out in the street," Merritt told him once she let go of the door handle. Since they were so close, she hadn't fastened her seat belt. *Not smart,* she told herself. "I hope you don't get stuck trying to turn around."

After braking parallel to where a snowdrift indicated the front steps should be, Cain said, "I'm hoping to avoid that."

Confused, Merritt ventured a questioning look.

"Would it make you uneasy if I parked in the barn tonight?"

He couldn't be serious. "It's filthy and probably full of rodents. Plus there's no heat in there. With all of the cracked boards and critter holes, it'll probably feel like a wind tunnel."

"I picked up a blanket at the dollar store. It'll be all right."

She didn't think one would be enough. "What do I tell Alvie when I find you dead in the morning?"

"You're the one who keeps risking exposure to the cold. Anyway, why do you have to say anything?"

"Because it's her property."

"As you pointed out, it's a barn that's been allowed to fall into disrepair," Cain argued. "What will she care? It's not like I'm asking to sleep in the house with you. Do I have to draw you a picture? You're safe from me."

Great, she thought. Rub it in her face. He'd already made it clear how undesirable she was. "You know what?" she said and grabbed the tote with one hand and the handle with the other. "Do what you want."

After she slid off the seat into the snow, she slammed the door shut and circled behind the vehicle to plow her way to the house. She didn't look back. The barn wasn't locked. He could deal with opening the double doors and making space for the truck by himself.

Once she shook off as much snow as possible and

got inside, she set down the tote and peeled off her outerwear. She left the shawl and coat on the entryway throw rug to avoid dealing with wiping up melted snow throughout the house.

"Pain in the backside, man," she muttered, attacking her boots. That's what she got for showing concern. Insults.

She continued on to the kitchen in her socks. There she set the tote on the counter and pulled on the thick-soled sneakers she wore as slippers. Annoyed with Cain as she was, she did turn on the back porch light. It had nothing to do with him, she assured herself. She would do it for anyone because it would be impossible to see inside the barn without it. What's more, he couldn't very well keep on the truck's headlights all night. What he would learn is that there was a side window that faced the house, and the porch light would filter through. For all of his know-it-all attitude, she doubted he'd thought of buying a flashlight when he'd purchased the blanket.

After putting on the kettle to make herself a hot mug of tea, Merritt went to get the stove fire going again. When lively flames were visible through the smoke-stained glass, she moved on to say hello to Wanda and Willy.

"Told you that I'd be back. Sorry to be late. You wouldn't believe the storm going on outside, but I'll bet the wind has had your attention." The old house creaked and groaned like some makeshift percussion instrument when these systems blew through. "I'll put on some music to block it out. I could use some soothing sounds myself."

Collecting her clothing and boots, Merritt hung the jacket and shawl on hooks by the back door and set her boots on a stool. Next, as promised, she turned on the small cassette player she'd found at a garage sale some months into her journey west. It had come with a plastic bag full of classical music. Obsolete tapes—which explained why everything was so cheap. She'd rarely had the luxury of listening to music while growing up, except what was played in school. Whomever her mother hooked up with seemed to like music at the bars well enough, but at home, they wanted silence—or, rather, *her* silent. Funny how they didn't return the consideration when they were three sheets to the wind and wanted to continue partying. At any rate, Merritt had no idea who half of the composers in the collection were, but she found the music as enthralling as Willy and Wanda seemed to.

Once she had her tea made, she went to sit for a few minutes by the aquarium. She enjoyed watching the fish do rhythmic laps around the tank during certain songs. That sent the plants swaying. She loved the bold tropical colors of the fish, coral and the plants, too. The aquarium had been sitting empty when she'd moved in. Merritt suspected it had belonged to Alvie's young daughter, although other than giving her permission to use it, Alvie never referred to it again.

Coming to the last sip of tea, Merritt forced herself out of the rocking chair. "Enjoy, you two. I have to get to work before I get lazy and fall asleep."

Back in the kitchen, she decided to work on the fried pies, which she would set on trays in the refrigerator overnight and deep-fry first thing in the morning. Once the dough was cooling in the fridge, she started on the chocolate filling for the variety that Sam Hughes had requested. She had canned apple and peach compote from local fruit harvested earlier in the year, so while the chocolate cooled, she started rolling out the dough and making pies with the fruit.

When those were all done and back in the cooler, she made a triple batch of corn bread muffins.

She was finishing with the cleaning up and trying to stifle repeated yawns when she heard a funny *crack-swoosh* sound. Certain that it had come from outside, she went to the back door wondering if the ancient oak tilting toward the west had finally come down under the weight of the snow.

Peering through the storm door, she could see the tree was intact, but the glass fogged up so much she couldn't see the rest of the yard. She unlocked the door, then opened it a slit so she could look farther. What she saw had her gasping.

The barn roof had collapsed.

"Dear God...he's buried alive!"

Chapter Three

Merritt shoved her feet into boots and dragged on her coat with equal desperation. Ignoring the shawl, which she figured would only be in the way, she snatched up the flashlight and shoved at the storm door that the wind tried to keep shut. She was slowed by the steep steps, and further by the iced-over iron handrail. Gloves would have made the descent less painful, but she hadn't taken the time to pull them on.

She was concerned with how badly the roof had damaged the truck and, as a result, how much air Cain had in the cab. Dare she hope that he had been outside of it when the collapse had occurred? But then he might have been struck by a beam.

The wind and snow lashed at her face. She slipped and fell, then fell again. But she finally reached the barn where she faced the next dilemma—the doors were barred from the inside. Of course! Once he'd pulled the truck inside, dropping the metal bar on the inside braces would be the only way to keep the wind from blowing everything wide open.

"Cain!" she screamed in fear and frustration.

There was a side door. She had used it earlier to bring the cats the warm milk. The knob turned when she twisted it, but the door itself didn't yield. Had he locked it? Why? Then it struck her that in the cave-in, something could have fallen against the door.

"No!" she cried, twisting again and pushing. She was the wrong person for this. Shifting to place her shoulder against the wood, she thrust again…and again. After several tries, the door yielded maybe six or eight inches. Enough for her to stick her head inside.

What she saw could have been a scene out of a sci-fi movie. The barn looked like it had a cave built in the middle of it. In the beam of her flashlight snow and dust spilled down from the sky like diamond flakes. That was the end of the beauty. The truck, she saw with growing despair, was all but covered with snow and debris except for the very end of the bed.

Of the cats, she saw and heard nothing. *How eerie,* she thought. Except for the wind outside, it was deathly quiet.

"Cain?" She checked the ground and saw a stack of sacks had fallen and one was against the door. Pushing again, she managed to get a few more inches of leeway to ease inside. Then she shoved the bag out of her way and gingerly stepped over the rest of the pile.

She approached the truck to see what she could through the passenger window. The cab was filled, too. "Can you hear me? Hold on! I'm getting you out!"

She had never said anything more ludicrous. With the windshield smashed and that weighty pile on the roof of the cab, maybe the roof had been smashed in, too.

The mass was a bizarre sculpture, like a mangled beast that had crashed to earth. Beams nailed to beams had twisted in their collapse, taking on human formations. Merritt's shocked mind saw a bent arm in the jagged remains of the windshield, and a giant leg arching high over the cab and coming to rest on one side of the bed. She couldn't do anything with those big beams. But she did manage to figure out where the driver's door was and brushed and pulled away debris to gain access to the latch. But there was way too much weight on top and it wouldn't open no matter how hard she tugged at it. He would suffocate before she reached him.

"Cain? I can't get the door open. The frame may be bent. Is there any way you're able to help? How badly are you hurt?"

She thought she heard a mumble or a moan. In any case, it was indecipherable.

"Please—stay awake. Help me!"

"See your light. Stand back," he said, his voice slightly stronger.

She did—or she thought she had given him adequate space. But when he gave a mighty kick, the door burst open…and caught her with enough force to send her flying off her feet. It seemed to happen in slow motion, at least slow enough for her to conclude she was about to become permanently welded to whatever she landed on. Fortunately, she fell into more bags of feed or fertilizer, she'd never lingered in the place long enough to determine which, but they were hardened enough that the connection was a harsh body blow that reverberated through every last nerve ending.

Weak and winded, she slid like drying cement to the dirt floor. She didn't think she could take much more—that was until she saw what Cain was still dealing with. He was having to twist and inch himself from the tiny tunnel he was creating with his body on the front bench seat. That gave her the strength to drag herself to her feet and grab boot, hand, jacket…whatever she could to assist him.

Finally, he was freed. He collapsed onto the packed dirt floor, his momentum and weight taking her down again. They lay there in a heap, him panting, her exhaustion compounded by his weight, yet relieved that despite her previous annoyance with him, he had survived.

"I hate to rush you," she wheezed. "But could you at least roll over a bit? I think my ribs are about to pierce my lungs."

Grunting, he did as she'd asked, ending up flat on his back. That allowed Merritt to drag herself to her knees, relocate the flashlight and check on him.

"Oh, no…you're bleeding."

As she dug into her pocket for the tissues she usually carried, she told herself not to panic at the amount of blood. She'd heard that head injuries always produced significant flow but she hoped his were minor. As the beam of her light closed in on the gash on his right temple, she saw the cut was bad enough to need stitches. They had no way to get to the hospital or to call for help. "Here." She shoved the tissues into his hand and brought it to the wound. "Hold this and press. We have to stem the flow of blood. Damn...I'll bet this means you have a concussion. Do you know who you are and where you are?"

He kept his eyes closed against the light, but said, "Unfortunately, yes."

"Do you know who I am?"

"Yes."

What else was she supposed to do? Check for even dilation, but she wasn't going to waste precious time doing that out here. Who knew if the rest of the barn's roof would hold?

"Keep pressing. I need to make sure there's not more bleeding." She put down the flashlight and gingerly slid her fingers through his hair, searching for any injury that would make moving him dangerous. "I think you're all right. How's your vision? You have a funny look on your face. Please tell me you can see okay."

With the light off of him, he had been watching her. His expression suggested that he thought her a figment of his imagination.

"Cain. Stop trying to scare me. Speak."

Just as she was about to hold up two fingers and ask him how many he saw, he framed her face within his hands and drew her down for a kiss. It was the one reaction that Merritt hadn't been expecting. On the other hand, it wasn't one of Dennis's sloppy, drunken attempts with an instant assault into her mouth. Nor was her impulse to immediately gag in offense. Oh, no, it wasn't. His kiss was astonishingly skillful and delicious, and it spread a pleasure that stole reasonable thought away as it seduced and invited.

Inevitably, helplessly, her body responded. Deprived of any tenderness for years, it wanted more, and when he took hold of her upper arms and drew her completely onto his torso, she went. The intimate contact awakened nerve endings she didn't know she possessed and filled her with a keen desire. This was what it *should* feel like, she realized as she instinctively tightened her legs around the thigh thrust between hers. Her hips wanted to rock, her tongue wanted to stroke, her nipples didn't just want his fingers, they wanted his mouth.

Fingers?

As her mind caught up with her body, she realized he had one hand inside her jacket and was stroking her through her thin sweater. Panicked, she did the first thing that came to mind—she bit his lip.

Cain uttered a guttural howl and brushed her aside like a feverish man would an offending blanket—and just as easily. "What the hell is wrong with you?" he snapped.

Crab-walking backward until she could brace herself against the stack of feed, Merritt gave as good as she got. "Me? What do you think you're doing?"

He glared at her as she climbed to her feet, all the while rubbing his bitten lip. Then slowly, the glare vanished, and he eyed his fingers with consternation. With a sigh, he sat up.

"I guess that knock on the head did away with what sense I had left."

"The tissues are on your lap," she told him with

schoolmarm sternness. "Hold them to that gash before you lose too much blood to walk."

He did as she directed. "Are you okay?"

Was he kidding? She wanted to scream at him. Her body and mind's betrayal made sarcasm rise like bile in her and she wanted to say, *Sure, and thanks for getting aroused without needing to pinch and punish, and for not reeking of booze and poor hygiene.*

"Merritt?"

With superhuman will, she pushed down her old hurt and spontaneous reactions. "Let's get you to the house." Like a storm survivor, she felt caught in an out-of-body experience—until she moved. Each step won a wince from her and she hoped he was strong enough to navigate through the snow under his own power because her body was acting like she'd gone down another flight of stairs.

He proved he could at least stand without wobbling.

Merritt glanced around. "Is there anything you need at the moment?"

"This, I guess." He started tugging on one end of the blanket, which had partially come out of the hole with him, until it hung on something.

"Leave it before it rips," she told him. "I have more."

She started for the side door, only to realize he wasn't following. Merritt turned around and saw he was inspecting the mess that had fallen on him as though seeing it for the first time.

"Do you think the truck is a total loss?" she asked.

"It was a piece of junk when I bought it, but what I'd earned while in prison and what I had on me when arrested couldn't buy much. It sure wasn't worth insuring, even if I'd had the money for more than liability coverage."

"Then come on before the rest of the building collapses."

This time, she limped off without looking back. Before she'd gotten too far, she heard the telltale crunch of snow behind her, indicating that he'd decided to follow. As she climbed the stairs, her foot slid off the second step. Cain's hands immediately gripped her by the waist to steady her.

She accepted that his strength and speed were a mixed blessing, given what had just happened in the barn, and murmured, "Thanks."

Inside the house, she let him pass, then closed and locked the doors against the wind and driving snow. "Have a seat," she instructed as she peeled off her jacket. By the time she had removed her boots, he had lowered himself into a chair. He otherwise acted uncertain.

If he was feeling guilty, good, she thought, taking the bloody mass of tissues from him and throwing them into the trash bin by the door. It looked like the bleeding had slowed, so she dealt with helping him out of his denim jacket and T-shirt next. Both were covered with blood and would require soaking before washing. For the moment, she didn't try to deal with his worn, black Western-style boots and went for a pan of warm water to which she added antiseptic liquid detergent. Collecting two clean washcloths and a dish towel from drawers beside the sink, she wet the first cloth and placed it against the wound.

"Hold again," she directed.

While he did that, she wet the second cloth and blotted up as much blood as she could, even wiping at where it was caking in his hair. Once satisfied that the bleeding had stopped, she took his cloth and put both into the pan.

"This is probably a twelve- or fifteen-stitch wound, but we can try a pressure bandage and hope it will hold." Considering the company her mother had kept, Merritt had witnessed her share of wounds caused by falls and fights.

"It's cheaper than the E.R. we can't get to, and it's not like it'll be my first scar."

Yes, he did have a slash at his chin, but it was faded and only added to his rugged sensuality. Were there other souvenirs of a hard life? As her gaze helplessly roamed over his weight lifter's pecs and arms, she murmured, "I'll be right back with everything."

She collected what she needed and set it all on the dining table. She then finished cleansing his face, particularly the wound area, using cotton balls dipped in hydrogen peroxide. Occasionally, she caught him risking a glance at her, but for the most part he kept his eyes closed.

After one deep sigh from him, she defended herself. "I'm trying to be as careful as I can."

"That wasn't a complaint. Your touch is like the brush of a moth wing."

She couldn't help but grimace.

"What now? That was a compliment."

"Alvie calls me Miller Moth. I'm sure she thinks that's a compliment, too."

"You are little."

"Little, insignificant, thanks. I've got it."

He uttered a brief, dry laugh. "About as insignificant as this pain in my head. You may appear quiet and harmless, but you pack a sting, sweetheart. In more ways than one."

Merritt hadn't meant it the way he took it, but she wasn't sure his description of her personality was anything to be encouraged about. Determined to finish so she could put some distance between them, she carefully added the antibiotic ointment.

"Ah," Cain said with sudden revelation. "You don't mean insignificant as in intelligence and temperament. You meant looks."

"You know, I'm trying to finish up here so that I can get to bed. Morning for me starts at four o'clock at the latest."

"Chicken," he murmured, the hint of amusement flickering in his eyes. "If you'd have let me finish telling you why I sighed, you wouldn't be wasting your time complaining about one little word so much." The amusement vanished and he grew serious. "I was going to say that I'm not sorry for kissing you. That would make me either a liar or a block of wood. But I am sorry that now you can't bring yourself to trust me."

Did he think her gullible and a fool? "Don't take it personally. I've lost the ability to trust anyone."

"I know." He moved his hand in an inclusive way between them. "On some unspoken level we recognize that in each other. That's why I have to give you something."

"Give me...?" Her instinctive suspiciousness triggered alarm. "You're not going to give me a dead bird's feather or something, are you? Obviously, you're Indian—pardon, Native American. Alvie said Sioux?"

"On my mother's side, but I'm a product of my father's culture, as well. Merritt, this isn't about the energy from totem animals or lucky charms."

"Okay, good."

"But I don't want to carry the image of you fearing me in my mind…or the weight of it on my soul. So I need you to accept."

"What?"

"My word."

No wonder the men in town were worried about their daughters and sweethearts being around this man. Even his assurances were charismatic. "You went through all of this when you could have said, 'Merritt, I'm going to make you a promise'?" she asked, her tone skeptical.

"People use the word *promise* all the time, to the point it means almost nothing to them."

He had a point. "And you think you're different?"

"I know so."

For once, she would love to see truth in advertising. "All right. Say what you want to say to ease my—" she couldn't make herself use the word *fear* "—concern about you."

He waited until she relented and met his gaze. Then he said quietly, "I would never take from you what you wouldn't want me to have."

That was it?

After several seconds, Merritt finished opening the bandage. The continued slight unsteadiness in her hands gave away her inner turmoil and caused her to drop part of the wrapping. She was glad for the cloak of busyness.

He meant well, she accepted that, but he couldn't know how many times she'd been assured that she was safe and that she had a protector, a guardian, only to learn that person was the most serious threat to her. No, he didn't understand. How could he? *He* was a man. The power was theirs. Always.

"How long have you had that condition with your hands?" Cain asked quietly, breaking into her thoughts.

Merritt thought time and a lot of inner work had made her shaking less noticeable. As she placed the first bandage over the wound, she should have known from the stillness she'd witnessed from observing him several times today that he would be more observant than most. She needed a moment to decide if he had a right to know her truth. Was he at least politely compassionate, or someone who was harvesting information to play someone he saw as a challenge and temporary entertainment?

"Pretty much for as long as I can remember," she finally told him. "And it comes and goes. I was also always cold as a kid and we were poor, so sometimes I could explain it away as being related to a chill."

No one knew about her past, not even Alvie, except to have been told that she had no one left back home. Opening up to Cain would go against how she'd operated since leaving New Jersey. Even longer. But he said they had trust issues in common. She believed that considering what Alvie had said about why he'd been sent to prison.

"Okay," she said, making a decision. "But this is

between us, deal? Alvie thinks the reason I don't talk about family or go see anyone is because I'm orphaned, which is only half right. Well, I don't know if my father is dead or not, but I guess if I don't know, it doesn't matter anyway."

Cain waited.

"I tried to love my mother," Merritt began. "She was creative and when straight and sober, she could be wonderfully funny. But after my father left her...us... she never was sober enough to make smart or healthy choices in her life."

"And those choices hurt you as much as they did her."

"That's why they call it baggage." She opened another bandage and secured it below the first strip. It didn't completely close the gash, but it was an improvement.

"The last guy in her life materialized during my senior year in high school. Stanley had a clone son named Dennis, who was alternately mean when Stan was drunk, and drunk when Stanley was mean. In between, Dennis was a pervert. I had to move my entire chest of drawers against the door at night to get any sleep and timed my showers around his absences."

"Is he who you have to thank for your hip?"

"You don't get points for lucky guesses," she quipped. When his face remained expressionless, Merritt averted her gaze and continued, "This was in Jersey where just about every house involves stairs. He came home one morning when I was running late getting out of the shower. He grabbed me and, long story short, I went down a whole flight trying to get away from him. I suppose I'm lucky that I didn't break my neck."

Cain closed his eyes briefly. "I take it you couldn't afford to go to a hospital any more than I could?"

"In fact, I did go. After I tried to go to school, only to faint on the front sidewalk. A neighbor saw me and called 911. That's when a doctor told me I needed surgery."

"It strikes me that child services would have been brought in just as a precaution. You were still a minor at what? Seventeen?"

"Barely. And we're talking Jersey. Overwhelmed hospital. Not so good neighborhood."

"How old was menacing Dennis compared to you?"

"He was twenty-one at the time. His father's *pal*. What happened to me was just a misunderstanding."

"Did you manage to finish school?" When she nodded, he continued, "After graduation you should have left."

She couldn't tell him how many times she started to. She'd been talking herself into it since she was eleven. "I wasn't strong or smart enough," was all she told Cain.

"Somehow I think that's the least truthful thing you've said tonight."

"I was twenty-three when Mother died," she said fast-forwarding the story. She couldn't defend what was indefensible even to her. "Mom begged me not to leave her" was a stupid, even suicidal excuse. "Her heart finally gave up from all the abuse. After the funeral, Stanley and Dennis went straight to their favorite bar.

I used that as my opportunity to pack and finally leave. Dennis arrived before I could.

"He was barely able to stand and started banging on my bedroom door. When he couldn't get it open, he left momentarily—I thought to get something to break the door down. I grabbed my bag and started to go out through the window. Then I heard a crash and afterward only silence. I discovered that he'd intended to fool me—slip out the bathroom window and use the first-floor roof to reach me through my bedroom window. But he'd lost his balance and struck the tub."

"He fractured his skull, I hope," Cain drawled.

"No, but he was bleeding. Worse than you were. Instead of helping him, I left," she said.

"Good for you."

She shook her head. "I took what money he had. It was enough to buy a bus ticket to Philadelphia, where I changed my appearance before buying another ticket to Baltimore. I started working where I could find a job, until people got too curious about me or I simply didn't feel like I could make a home in a place. Then I'd buy another bus ticket to somewhere else. After about a year of that, I got tired of cities and thought I'd try something else. Almost's city limit sign made me laugh out loud. But the way it was framed in the bus's window seemed like a message, too." Plucking at a torn bit of cuticle on her left thumb, she told him, "There may be a reward out for me. If you turned me in, you could probably get that windshield fixed and get someone to make both doors open like they should."

"It'll get fixed," Cain said quietly. "Have you considered that there may be no reason for you to worry?

Maybe you're cheating yourself out of the life you deserve for nothing."

"I'm living the life I deserve. I'm doing something I enjoy, in beautiful country. People are decent to me and the rest respect my privacy. I'm content."

Cain gestured at her hands. "Content people don't shake like they're plugged to a 110 outlet."

"So I'm a work in progress."

"And the baking hides the trembling. Or, rather, it's therapy."

"You reason pretty well for someone who may have a concussion."

"I'm glad for you. But it's a pity you haven't met someone in all this time that would appreciate all you are and encourage you to spread your wings even more. A marriage-or-nothing kind of woman is a treasure, especially in these times."

Marriage or nothing? "You're crediting me with virtues I don't possess. I haven't gotten involved with anyone because I haven't wanted to. Plain and simple. Frankly, if I loved you—I mean if I… For someone—it wouldn't matter if marriage was an option or not."

"Brave words, now that I've given you my word you're safe from me," he said, a flicker of teasing in his dark eyes.

His playfulness and the amusement in his expression caused a hitch in Merritt's chest. So much for trying to act mature about her sexuality when, the truth was, she had less experience than some girls a decade her junior—or younger. Self-conscious, she scooped up his clothes. "It's getting late. I need to soak these before I put them in the washer and dryer. While they're in the tub, I'll get you a pallet made on the couch."

"You're sure you're okay with that?"

Merritt considered his question with the somberness it deserved. "You had plenty of opportunity to hurt me before the roof fell on you. Besides, it's not like there's much option. You're in no condition to brave the weather to get to town. Do you want milk or water with the painkiller for your throbbing head?" she added, heading for the medicine chest.

Chapter Four

When Merritt next opened her eyes, it was still dark outside, very quiet and cold. Usually, she left the bedroom door open so she could benefit from the stove's heat, but common sense and modesty had compelled her to shut and lock it.

She hated the thought of leaving the warmth of the thick quilt and microfiber blanket, but she forced herself to push back the covers. Her feet in heavy socks, she sought her sneakers on the throw rug beside the bed. Then she reached for her black fleece robe to pull over her red flannel pajamas.

Her bedside clock indicated it was almost a quarter after four o'clock. She never set the thing because she always woke when she needed to. Her inner clock had betrayed her. She wasn't all that surprised, considering yesterday's exertion and stress, but now running late, she had to move faster than usual to make it to the café for their six o'clock opening. How was the weather now?

At the door, she listened for any sound that Cain was already up. There was no reason except that the couch was a little short for him and not the most comfortable thing for a man his size. After easing back the slide lock, she turned the knob and opened the door, thinking she would try to tiptoe out and at least manage her shower before any noise woke him. If he woke, she would fry the pies here. If he slept, she would fry them at the restaurant.

Light greeted her, but no Cain. She circled the living room to find his bedding was nicely folded and placed in the middle of the couch.

The light she'd first noticed was from the kitchen, but he wasn't there either, and the bathroom was empty. His jeans jacket and T-shirt were gone from the dryer where she'd had them drying when she went to bed. She'd asked for the jeans once he'd gotten under the covers. She'd noticed blood on them, too.

Now what? she wondered. Had he left? How? His truck was buried and not drivable.

She went to the front window and, thanks to the porch light, saw the good news that it had stopped snowing. She also realized that Cain must have been up for a while because the porch stairs were cleaned off and a shovel-wide trail had been dug to the dirt driveway and out to the road. She had a feeling the back stairs were clear, too. Glancing back toward the barn, she spotted what looked like a lantern light and heard the faint rumble of a motor.

Cain was in the garage trying to free his truck.

Could his intent be to help her get to town? It was a miracle the engine had turned over considering her last image of the vehicle.

As touched as she was ashamed for her security precautions, she was tempted to dress and hurry out to offer her help. It was risky for him to take on such a project after yesterday's injury. But accepting that she had a commitment to Alvie, she went to have a quick shower while she had the house to herself. Old habits die hard, she admitted to herself, thinking of her confession to Cain yesterday.

By the time she was dressed in clean jeans and her latest addition to her sparse wardrobe—an orange sweater with a pumpkin and scarecrow appliqué ironed on the front—she had a pot of coffee made and the pies frying. When she was well into her second batch, she heard the front door open and shut.

Looking frozen and like he hadn't slept more than a few minutes, Cain came to the kitchen rubbing and blowing on his hands. "It won't be fun," he began, "but I can get you to town. I got the cab cleaned out, and there shouldn't be any shards of glass flying at us from what's left of the windshield. Most importantly, the engine is still running and I can get at least the driver's door open and shut."

Merritt left the deep fryer to pour steaming coffee into the mug she'd already taken out for him when she'd gotten hers. "What if the rest of the roof came down on you or you fell while doing all of that?"

"Well, it didn't. I didn't."

"You're acting like you did get a concussion," she continued, her concern for him provoking her. "And you look like a train dragged you from Montana to Idaho and back."

"Good morning to you, too."

The slow, drawn-out greeting got to her as much as the disappointment in his eyes for her lack of appreciation for his achievement. Merritt slid the coffee across the counter, feeling more than a little chagrin.

"Good morning," she said, more subdued. "I apologize. Obviously, I'm not used to such gestures." She motioned to the kitchen table. "I'll get you breakfast at the café, but would you like to sit down and have a fresh chocolate fried pie with your coffee? You really do look like you should take a break. There'll be apple and peach shortly, if you prefer."

Cain unbuttoned his jacket. Sliding it off, he hung it over the back of the chair on the end of the table, then came for the coffee. Merritt was glad to see the stains had come out of his clothes, especially the T-shirt, and couldn't help but admire how the soft material caressed his broad shoulders and toned abdomen.

"Chocolate will be great, thanks," he said. "I could smell them and the coffee all the way at the barn. It's a wonder you haven't wakened some hungry bear from his hibernation."

Placing the pastry on a plate, she plucked off two lengths of paper towels and handed that to him. "Don't say that. I'm not sure either of those back doors are sturdy enough to withstand a bear's determination or temper. You'll have me thinking those inside shutters in the living room aren't just to keep the house warmer in a blizzard, as Alvie said."

As Cain accepted the plate, their fingers brushed

against each other and a current of awareness and heat jolted Merritt. The way his gaze momentarily locked with hers told her that he'd felt something, too.

No sooner did he put down his coffee than he lifted a pastry to his mouth.

"Oh, wait!" she cried. "Be careful with that first bite. It takes a while for the insides to cool."

"I'm glad you warned me." He tore the pastry in two. "I'm so hungry, I was about to stick half in my mouth straight off." He took a cautious bite, then a larger one, which was followed by a moan of pleasure. "This should be illegal."

Delighted, Merritt stopped flipping pies and watched him devour her concoction. "Really?"

"Lady, you are gifted. I'm guessing that's not instant pudding?"

She chuckled. "Not hardly." Returning her attention to the fryer, she basked in the glow of his praise. She'd thought more than once about taking some culinary courses, then talked herself out of it. Since she wasn't in a metropolitan area these days, she'd stopped fantasizing.

"You didn't say if you got any sleep?" Cain asked.

"That's my line, albeit in a roundabout way, which you ignored."

"I can get at least forty winks anywhere. What about you? You're the one who had a stranger in her house. Did the slide bolt reassure you?"

Merritt could feel her face sting with embarrassment. "I tried to be quiet so as not to offend you."

"You did what you needed to do for you."

"That's something someone who hadn't been around

you for the last day would say. But I don't have that excuse. Especially not after you gave me your word."

"Gave it, but understood that you would accept it only when you were ready."

Merritt shook her head. "How did someone who talks like you do get a name like Cain? Was your poor mother on too strong pain medication and chose the wrong biblical name?"

"My grandfather named me."

Sanford Paxton himself? "He punished you just because he didn't want to accept your father had gotten your mother pregnant?"

"Tom and Lily were in love. But my father died in an accident at the ranch before he could marry my mother. He was crushed by his horse in a fall. My grandfather knew of my father's intent, but at the funeral, he made it clear to my mother that he wouldn't acknowledge or support any child she bore."

"She must have been terrified of the prospect of becoming a single parent," Merritt said, thinking of a beautiful, feminine version of Cain.

"Her mother, my grandmother, stuck by her, but they were pretty much outcasts on the reservation." Cain carried his dishes to the sink. "You already know that my mother died during childbirth. What you apparently didn't hear through the gossip mill is that after they lifted me out during the cesarean procedure, they discovered my twin brother was already dead."

"No," Merritt whispered. "How tragic."

"Somehow the umbilical cord got wrapped around his neck. As the story goes, Sanford had been called into the hospital. He supposedly looked at me and my dead brother and pointed at me, saying, 'Name that one Cain and send him home to his grandmother.'"

It was a good thing that Merritt was finished with the fried pies, because she couldn't focus on anything for the horror she'd just heard. She angrily pulled the cord from the outlet. "How could he?" she cried.

Cain returned to the chair and pushed it in, then picked up his jacket. "You'll have to ask him."

"That's not likely to happen," she replied. "Most of the time when he comes into the café, he sits with a group of ranchers in Nikki's area. Once or twice I topped off his coffee mug and he murmured his thanks, but that's about it. I'm sure he wouldn't recognize me if our paths crossed on the street." Merritt couldn't help but ask, "Have you ever talked to him over the years?"

"No." After several seconds, he allowed, "Our paths have crossed, too. Enough for me to know he's aware of who I am, but refuses to acknowledge it."

"I was afraid of that." What on earth happened in his life that made him feel justified to inflict such pain in someone else's? His son's child, no less. Once again she thought about how Cain had ended up in prison. "He's soulless. He had to know who really beat— Who was the foreman at the ranch before Josh Bevans?"

"Dane Jones."

"Yet he let you be framed."

"It would appear that way, but I can't prove it."

"Whatever happened to Dane?"

"Someone at the reservation told me he left or quit shortly after I was sent away and enlisted. He was killed in Afghanistan last year."

"Wow." It sounded like he had more of a conscience

than Sanford Paxton did. Merritt wanted to ask more questions, but caught sight of the clock. She groaned in regret. "I have to get all of this packed and get moving."

"I'll take it out to the truck when you're ready," Cain told her. "While you finish up with whatever you need to do before leaving."

"What about your head? Do you think you should take another pain pill? Better yet, take the bottle for whenever you need another."

"I'm not one for pills. I think the worst is over."

"At the very least, you need to let me replace those bandages. You need another dose of antibiotic ointment and one of the bandages is loose on one end."

Despite thinking they'd made good time, it was minutes after six o'clock when Cain eased the truck down the driveway. He was right about it being an unpleasant ride, and Merritt was glad she had her shawl to cover her face from the biting wind, even though he wasn't going more than ten miles an hour. But what could one expect when it was barely eighteen degrees?

"I wish I had a muffler for you," she told him. He looked absolutely frozen, but at least he'd found a pair of work gloves to protect his hands from freezing to the steering wheel.

"I'll be fine. It's not like we're going far."

It turned out that they were still the first ones at the café, aside from Alvie and Leroy, so Cain parked right at the door. Alvie and Leroy went wide-eyed when they saw how Merritt had arrived and who helped her carry things inside. Merritt knew his battered condition only added to their consternation. After cleaning

Cain's gash and replacing the pressure bandages, she'd added a gauze pad over it all to protect the wound from possible splinter fragments or any other debris. Despite Cain's overlong hair often falling across his brow, the white gauze drew more attention.

Cain offered a quiet "good morning" to them and set Merritt's things on the end of the lunch counter closest to the kitchen. Then he backtracked to the table he'd sat at yesterday morning.

After a questioning glance at Merritt, Leroy shrugged and carried the tote in back where he set it on Merritt's usual workstation next to the upright cooler. She followed with the plastic containers bearing the fried pies and Alvie brought up the rear. As Merritt removed her outerwear and changed from boots to sneakers, the silence grew increasingly expectant.

"You're hair's wet," Alvie finally said.

There was nothing like stating the obvious, Merritt thought, grasping by her boss's chilly tone that she wasn't going to see any positive viewpoint no matter how logical Merritt explained things. "Sorry. I know it doesn't look professional, but there just wasn't time to wrestle with a blow-dryer this morning. Um…I see Nikki isn't here yet. Did she call to officially bow out of this morning's shift?"

"No call. I imagine she'll be a no-show, at least through morning. Especially if she has company. Speaking of which, I'm surprised by yours." With her chef's apron already on, Alvie went to the refrigerator and brought out eggs, a long roll of breakfast sausage, a package of bacon and a platter bearing half of a smoked ham.

Merritt paused midway in tying on her black apron to watch her as she set everything on the workstation beside the griddle. "I don't know that I deserve that, Alvie, considering that it's thanks to Cain that I'm here. And you saw how he looks. There's someone who deserves to be in bed. He was almost killed."

"Good grief, Miller Moth, do you mean he already got himself in a fight? After all this time presenting yourself as a quiet good girl, *that's* the kind of man you want to tie your reputation to?"

Merritt had never been on the receiving end of Alvie's censure or ire, and short of emptying the cash register and giving everything to Nikki, she didn't see how that could ever happen—until today. Although her insides were sinking, she hoped the woman who had given her a chance at a new life, and hope, would listen.

"He got hurt when the roof of *your* barn fell in on him," she began.

Alvie's shock rippled into guilt, but lasted only seconds. "Huh. Serves him right for sneaking in there."

"He didn't—" Taking a deep breath, Merritt corrected her. "There was no sneaking. I told him he could put the truck in there to get out of the weather after he gave me a lift home. He had to sleep somewhere."

Alvie seemed to only hear a conspiracy. "What? He hung around last night and waited for you? It sounds like he's stalking you! And to think I was one who defended him."

"You were right to do that, Alvie. He stayed in town out of consideration. Do you think he enjoys being gawked at by everyone? He could have driven to the house and waited for me there, but he didn't. He showed concern about me walking home in that storm. I didn't see anyone else doing that."

Obviously aware that she was referring to Leroy, Alvie grew more agitated and her chest heaved as she struggled for a worthy reply. When none came, she snapped, "You're softer than a pad of butter dropped on this griddle."

Knowing she'd won that round on common sense, Merritt was gracious. "You would have done the same."

"I'm not twentysomething with the life experience of a sixteen-year-old."

Alvie's inability to take the olive branch hurt. So did hearing how she was really perceived. "The roof collapsed," she reiterated with quiet dignity. "You're unhappy with me. I get that. But once I heard the crash, what was I supposed to do, ignore it?" Merritt forgot all about unpacking the tote and starting the breadbaskets. She even forgot that Cain was waiting for her to bring him coffee and take his order. "I tell you, Alvie, when I first got the stuck door open from the junk that had fallen against it in the crash, I thought he was dead. The debris—snow, timber, everything—was all over that truck. Go outside and look at it more closely. It's cleaned up now because he was up all hours doing that and clearing the snow from around the house so I could walk easier. But the windshield is gone and the passenger door won't open. That bandage on his head? That's covering a gash that should have at least a dozen stitches. Maybe twenty."

On the defensive now, Alvie put her hands on her hips. "Why didn't he get them?"

"How? We couldn't exactly call 911. His only option was to walk in that blizzard to the police station, but I doubt he would have made it. I was that scared that he was concussed or would bleed to death."

But all Alvie did was narrow her eyes. "So you nursed him."

"Of course I did."

"And he slept where?"

That was it, Merritt thought. This wasn't about Cain being hurt, this was about Alvie unwilling to admit she was wrong. "On the couch," she replied quietly.

The older woman snatched up the spatula and slapped it on the stainless steel work counter. "How dare you abuse my goodwill! That's my grandmother's house, not to be turned into a— Shame on you. There are *gentlemen* in this town who would court you proper if you would give them a chance. But no, you, who pretends to be too shy to say more than a half dozen words to a customer, takes up with a convict before he's even washed the smell of prison off himself!"

Her reckless conclusions won a gasp from Merritt, who backed away from the vitriol as though the toxicity was venom. Backed right into a wall. No, she amended when strong hands gripped her upper arms to steady her. She spun around to see Cain looking as grim as she'd ever seen him.

As he began to speak, she laid her hand against his chest, signaling him to please say nothing. Then she looked over her shoulder at Alvie.

"I did nothing wrong. I only did what any decent person with a conscience would do, and if you can't grasp that, then I guess we have nothing more to discuss. I'm done here." She ripped off the apron and flung it down on the counter on her way to get her things. Not wanting to linger a second longer than she had to, for fear of losing the shaky grip on her control, she held them against her and said to Cain, "Let's go."

"Let me talk to her."

"No. There's been more than enough said."

The only reason Cain let Merritt urge him out of there was because he could see what Alvie's rant was costing her. He knew Alvie needed a dose of her own medicine, and he deserved to clear his name, but he wasn't going to let Merritt take two steps back psychologically after all of the hard-won ground she'd reclaimed for herself.

They left as a customer Cain didn't recognize came to the door shivering and stomping snow off of his boots. He began to smile at Merritt, then looked confused as he realized she was leaving. No doubt one of her regulars. He hoped Leroy, and Alvie, got laryngitis from trying to cover why their best waitress wasn't there.

He wasn't surprised at Alvie's overreaction. Under different circumstances—if it had been Nikki who'd offered him a place to sleep—Alvie would have pretty much taken it in stride. But this had been different. No doubt Alvie felt as though her favorite, her precious surrogate daughter, was in danger of being lured away by someone Alvie saw as a wolf—one who had been wrongfully caged, true, but was now free, to the public's detriment. She wouldn't stand by and lose another piece of her heart.

If only she hadn't jumped to conclusions, he would have eased her mind. He would have told her, *I understand. I'm going.*

The street remained a ghost of itself as Cain turned the truck back out of town. Occasional flurries fell from skies that remained overcast, and the emotional chill wasn't much better inside the cab. He knew Merritt was fighting tears, but she was resolved and refused to break down. Everyone had their breaking point, though, and he had picked up enough on her relationship with Alvie to know the older woman could have grown to become a mother figure in time. He needed to give that a chance to happen.

By the time they reached the house, Merritt still hadn't spoken. He parked to give her the easiest access to the front porch.

"Thank you," she said, her voice slightly husky. "If you'll come inside, I'll make you that breakfast."

Cain followed. He waited until they were inside and removing their jackets to put his decision into play. "What will you do now?" he asked.

"I don't know."

"That's because what you did wasn't smart. Noble, to an extent, but not your brightest move." At her disbelieving look, he kept on like a steamroller. "How will you make a living now? Except for the one-man taco shed operation on the other side of town, Alvie's the only restaurant here. Where will you stay, since you gave her every reason to evict you without any notice?"

Visibly upset, Merritt threw both shawl and jacket onto the nearest dining chair instead of hanging them up. "Quit. I know this."

"You didn't act like you did." He made himself cut a little deeper. "I don't need you to fight my battles, I already told you that."

"Did you expect me to stand by and let her insult both of us? Excuse me if I didn't handle things the way you wanted, but I'm sick and tired of being criticized for my inadequacies, and all but called stupid by the woman I called friend and mentor. So you'll have to excuse me if I don't feel up to being dissected and found wanting all over again."

"Wait a minute." As she spun away, Cain reached for her and forced her to turn back to him. Only she resisted and he overcompensated, which brought her breast to thigh against him. Whatever he'd planned to say, her sweet, clean scent and feminine form unraveled those good intensions, and his resistance. "Don't," he breathed, touching his lips to her forehead. "You're not any of those things. You're brave, and talented, and you're turning me inside out. So much so that I have to do this one last time."

There was no overpowering, no crushing kiss that might drive her into a panic. He had to say goodbye, he'd accepted that, but he wanted a perfect memory to take with him.

He touched his lips to the corner of her mouth, mostly because she turned away from him, then he applied the same tender caress to her cheekbone and her nose. When she turned to stare at him, he finally placed a soft kiss on the opposite corner of her mouth. Finally sensing he'd won her interest if not approval, he brushed his bruised lips against hers, again and again.

Inviting her to wrap her arms around his neck, he

slid his around her back and waist and continued tempting her with his lips and tongue to kiss him back. He had never been this careful with a woman, and would undoubtedly never touch anyone so gentle-spirited and good again. *Remember me in your heart, and take a little of mine into yours.*

As she opened for his deeper kiss, Cain groaned with pleasure. His body quickened, long-contained needs stirring every kind of hunger. Her mouth was like the first spring peach, her teeth dainty seed pearls, her tongue as shy as a fawn and as delightfully curious. He wanted her. But he was poison to her.

Forcing himself to put her at arms' length, he murmured, "Goodbye."

"What? Cain...you don't have to go."

He had a new memory—her eyes tender with invitation.

Cain nodded his head with regret. "Oh, yes, I do."

Then he quietly left her and shut the door behind himself.

An hour later, Merritt was still too stressed to sit for more than a second before she would leap up again and pace. Her ability to breathe was so-so, too. She knew what a panic attack was and figured she was as close as she'd ever been to one. One second twin streams of tears were pouring down her face without her uttering so much as a sniff, then a minute later the pressure was so bad to cry that every breath sounded ragged and hurt.

What had she done wrong? It just wasn't fair. For the first time she'd felt something for someone, and he'd left. Left her the day she'd also quit her job. For him. Could she make a better mess of things?

She was going to have to move. But how could she pack the fish? They'd die if left behind, either from cold or starvation. Alvie wouldn't want them. What's more, her money was in Alvie's safe. How humiliating that would be to go back there and ask for it. Surely Alvie would give it back to her. Merritt's mind was adept at thinking the worst because she'd seen the worst, and all of the what-ifs and to-dos were leaving her feeling sick to her stomach.

She had to lie down. *Just for a little while,* she assured herself as she collapsed onto the bed. As she pulled the quilt up to her chin, she felt the right decision would come to her. Something would come to her....

Knocking jerked her out of deep sleep. Disoriented, Merritt sat up too quickly and felt ill again, but the near darkness concerned her more. Had she slept all day? A glance at the clock told her that was true. It was after four o'clock!

As she quickly slid out of bed and hurried to the living room, she noticed how the cottage was getting cool. It had been hours since she'd tended the fire. With her luck there would be hardly any coals left to get a blaze going again.

Checking the window, she had another shock— Leroy's truck was out front. The thing had needed a new tire and a battery that didn't need charging every time he got behind the wheel. *Dear Lord,* she thought. That must mean he was here with instructions from Alvie to hurry her off the premises.

But when Merritt opened the door, she found that both them stood there. They looked as stressed by this ordeal as she felt.

"Who's managing the café?" was all that she could think to ask. But she did recover enough to step back to let them enter.

"It was the slowest day we've had since I opened the place," Alvie said, wringing her hands as she did when the weather made her arthritis act up. "Maybe the combination of the holiday next week and this weather convinced folks to count calories for a change and stay home. I don't know," she admitted in the next moment. "I just told Leroy it was an opportunity not to be missed. I said, 'Turn the sign and lock the door.'"

"Tell her the truth," Leroy said, his tone cajoling.

"What?" she asked a bit resentfully. "Okay, fine. First I told him to get that damned truck running."

"Before the breakfast traffic was even gone," Leroy said to Merritt with a speaking glance.

Merritt suspected that was to assure her of how anxious Alvie was to get here.

"What traffic?" Alvie muttered. "Three of your cronies growing roots on the lunch counter stools. I tended to them easily enough. The point is that I couldn't stand it," she told Merritt. "I wanted to talk to you." Pacing, Alvie got to the middle of the room and declared, "Honey, you can't quit. Granted, I got scared when I saw you with Cain. You know I've come to think of you as my own flesh and blood. I've even been dreaming that you take over the place once this arthritis gets the best of me."

Merritt continued to stand there with her arms

wrapped around herself from the chill as much as this latest bit of earth-rocking news. She supposed she should be thrilled. It was a relief to know how Alvie truly felt about her, and the opportunity to have her own place would be like a dream come true a decade or more early—if her past didn't intrude on her slowly evolving dreams. But, as Alvie was obviously doing, she had to reexamine things. Partly because of Cain, too.

"Well," she began. "I don't know what to say. I'm relieved and grateful that you're not angry with me anymore. But I can't deny what you said hurt deeply."

"Told you that you stuck your foot deep this time," Leroy said.

Alvie nudged him toward the stove. "The fire's gone out. You already had your opportunity to rub my nose in things."

"But it happens so rarely, I—"

"Leroy!"

As he walked away with a wink at Merritt, Alvie's expression turned to one of appeal.

"I know I wasn't being fair, but all I could think of was Cain getting into trouble again and dragging you down with him."

Merritt shook her head, needing to correct that. "It's wrong to say 'again.' His intent to seek justice for his uncle was misguided, sure. What you need to understand is that when he denied having beaten Dane Jones, he was telling the truth. Someone else did that. They just pinned it on Cain."

Alvie looked pained at her unwavering support of

Cain. "Hon, few people who end up in prison admit to being guilty."

"Believe it or not, I've known a few ex-cons and all of them combined don't add up to Cain in character." Seeing as that didn't make too much impact on Alvie, she tried a different approach. "Maybe you've forgotten—it had to have been spoken about around town—but even though Cain's hands weren't cut up, the sheriff believed Paxton Ranch witnesses over him. Doesn't that seem odd to you? Who told them to lie? Who else could have roughed up Sanford Paxton's foreman but another ranch hand? That begs the question why?"

Alvie looked away, clearly not happy with this subject.

"I think it's because Mr. Paxton himself wanted it that way," Merritt continued. "A good foreman must take some time to groom. He wouldn't want to lose him. And he wouldn't mind Cain being out of his sight because he reminded him of everything Mr. Paxton had lost. If you want to hold hard feelings for a Paxton, blame Sanford himself."

"I had hopes it would all turn out all right when Cain went into the service," Alvie said. "He so needed to get away from this place."

Merritt didn't think she could be surprised again, but Alvie proved her wrong. "Cain was in the military?"

"He was a marine. Went in at eighteen and did two stints. He should have stayed in. Maybe things wouldn't have turned out as they did."

Merritt pressed her hand to her head, reeling all over again from the thought of the injustices that had fallen on him. "How could Sanford treat his own flesh and blood that way? He named an innocent little boy one of the most despised names in the Bible. Can you imagine how Cain was treated in school? In the service?"

"Oh, they didn't want him to leave the service," Alvie said. "Like I told you, he was put up for a medal or something. They wanted him to make the service his life."

But he wanted to go home, Merritt thought. She suspected the military didn't fit any more than being an outcast to his own people did. "He didn't deserve to become the town's spittoon all over again," she ground out.

At that point Leroy cleared his throat as he rose from scooping out ashes from the stove. "I agree with you," he said. "But he didn't do himself any favors continuing to build on his reputation with the ladies. Hero or no hero, he was chased out of more than one henhouse, so to speak, by an irate daddy."

"I remember one being the mayor's daughter," Alvie told her. "Got caught in the girl's spanking-new, graduation-gift convertible. Breaking it in, so to speak. Marcie was shipped off to an all-girls' college on the East Coast. Never did come back here that I remember."

"There were a few ranchers' daughters, too," Leroy added. "They sure were wishing Sanford would claim the boy. Would've made their lives a whole lot easier if their daddies knew they had Sanford as their backup in more ways than one."

Although Merritt cringed inside at the thought of him with some of the most popular—and beautiful—

females in town, her sense of fairness stayed firm. "It's all so hypocritical. The girls could have been caught with the best quarterback in the district and their fathers would have happily arranged a wedding."

Sighing, Alvie said, "Be that as it may, just be careful about letting it be known that you and Cain both slept in the cottage, okay? Even if it was innocent. That could cost us a number of our churchgoing customers."

"Alvie, you and Leroy live together and that hasn't cost you any business."

"Oh, phooey," Alvie said with a dismissive wave. "That's because we're ancient. Nobody cares." The older woman looked hopeful. "Will you come back then? Will you think about my offer? The few who did show up asked about you. *You*—not Nikki. It's not just your baking people care about."

"I don't mean to sound like I'm holding out or anything, but I need to think through some things," Merritt admitted. "But I'd be happy to come back while I do that."

Alvie tried to take that with good grace. "I'll try not to bird-dog you." She gestured toward the outside. "I guess you can tell Cain that if he's looking for work, he might as well start by repairing that barn. You know I've tried to hire someone a few times, but I swear… the guys who want to work have jobs. The rest only do when their wives shove them out the door with a shotgun."

"Cain is gone." Merritt's throat grew as tight as when she'd heard his truck pull out of the yard earlier. "I don't think he intends to come back."

Chapter Five

Merritt did return to the café, and by the end of the week things seemed to return to normal. Maybe better in some ways. One positive was that Alvie dropped her gruffness around her and was less hesitant to show her affection. Merritt wasn't the only one who appreciated that. Leroy's sardonic personality sweetened as well now that his lady seemed more at peace.

As for Cain, although she tried, Merritt couldn't stop thinking about him. She certainly tried to stay busy to avoid fixating, even baking with new gusto. The result was that she'd had to stop taking Thanksgiving orders for pies and pumpkin tortes, since she'd worked herself into that much of a success. But at night, in bed, she couldn't stop reliving what it had been like to be held in his arms and kissed as though she was his last breath. Those memories even filtered into her dreams. It was driving her crazy. Better to have never been kissed at all, she decided, than to lie alone in her bed, aching and lonely.

The other negative was that she was seeing way too much of Sanford Paxton. He had come into the café two days in a row, and on Friday she had found him openly watching her. It had been later as she'd been walking home after the morning shift and he'd passed her coming from the opposite direction. She'd averted her gaze as he'd politely touched the brim of his Western hat, only to realize he was cutting a U-turn and returning to stop beside her.

The snow had melted off the road thanks to a subtle warm-up, and Merritt was trying desperately to walk without limping, sensing on some level what he was about to do. As he used the power key to lower the passenger window, she tensed with dread.

"Miss Miller, may I give you a lift the rest of the way home?" he asked, all chivalry.

How could he feel pity for her when he had none for his own flesh and blood? she thought with barely contained fury. Was he doing this because of something he'd noticed between her and Cain, or something Nikki said to him?

"No, thank you, sir," she managed, keeping her gaze on the highly polished passenger door handle. "I'm fine."

"Your courage is admirable, but clearly you're not fine. Please. I would feel better if you'd let me save you time and painful steps."

"Sir," she began, torn between loyalty and her sense of justice. "I'm trying to avoid making trouble for my employer, but I also have to tell you that you're wasting your time. I want nothing from you."

He looked surprised, then intrigued. Ironically, Merritt knew she'd seen that same expression on Cain's face.

"You don't like me…because of things you've heard."

She almost said, *Because of things I know.* However, she knew that would be going too far. "I'd rather not say anything else," she replied instead.

Her boldness had him raising his eyebrows; nevertheless, his mood remained steady. "You're stronger than you look. I suspected you might be. Good day to you, Miss Miller."

When she told Alvie later that day, she thought there was going to be a scene like the last one. Alvie turned a stack of boxed canned goods delivered moments before into a bench and sat down. Although pale, when she did speak, she was surprisingly calm.

"You were true to your beliefs and still respectful. I can't fault you for that."

"What if he never comes to the café again?" Merritt asked, hindsight adding to her worry. "What if he urges others to stop as well?

But the whole table was there the next day, including Sanford, and his attitude toward her was solicitous. That didn't sit well with Nikki.

"Trying to steal my customer?" she asked back in the kitchen.

"Don't be ridiculous," Merritt replied.

"You'd better not be or I'll make you lose one of yours."

* * *

The following Monday, Merritt was walking home as usual after her morning shift when she heard a truck coming from the direction of town. Her heart sank. *No,* she thought, stepping to the shoulder to give the vehicle wide berth. Sanford Paxton hadn't been in the café that morning; nevertheless, she didn't know anyone else who would be stopping for her.

When it pulled up beside her, she glanced over and stopped in her tracks.

Cain!

The truck had a shiny new windshield and the bed was filled with lumber. But what was the most amazing thing of all was that he'd gotten a haircut while he'd been gone. No more wild mane to be tossed by the wind; his glossy black hair was now smoothed into… Not a military bur, but conservative for him. He would never look like a lawyer or banker, and yet she was mesmerized by the change it made. She could see by the new black-and-white flannel shirt that he'd added to his wardrobe a bit, too.

He leaned across the seat and pushed the passenger door open.

"Want a ride?" he asked as though they'd seen each other only a few hours ago.

Buoyed by a euphoria she'd never known before, she wanted to draw out the moment a while longer. "It's not far and it's a pretty day. Besides, I wouldn't want to make you late for anything," she added, nodding to the lumber.

"You know damn well where this is going."

Unable to keep from smiling, Merritt settled the tote

on the floorboard and climbed in. A million and one questions came to mind, but she was willing to let him choose what to share and when. She was content just to know he was back.

Accelerating again, Cain said, "Don't get any ideas."

"Wouldn't think of it." Not surprised at his cautionary approach, she was determined to prove she was up to whatever he had in mind.

"I decided to do the repairs on the barn while I figure out what's next."

"Good for you. Nice haircut." She refused to ask questions, although her curiosity ran rampant.

"I guess if you're going to do contractor work, it helps not to scare the clients."

She noticed only one small bandage on his temple and minimal discoloration. "The cut is healing fast."

"Most of the time, I forget it's there. You did a good job nursing it."

It was nice of him to say so, but that wasn't what she wanted him to talk about. As he pulled into the driveway, she wondered when Alvie had hired him. Yesterday while she'd been home baking all day? Then where had he stayed last night? The thought that he might have hooked up with one of his past flames Alvie and Leroy had mentioned did bad things to her hopefulness.

"Why didn't you hold good on your threat and leave?" he asked. "You could do a lot better than Almost."

"I like it here," she said with a shrug. "Alvie told me she cares for me."

"You hadn't figured that out?"

"She admitted she needs me."

"Well, don't think that's contagious."

"I should be so unlucky." She sat so straight on the seat, she felt her spine was fused. "I appreciate the ride and however you managed to get back on Alvie's good side. I'm glad you have some work, but believe me, you're safe from me."

"Is that so?"

As soon as Cain stopped in the driveway, Merritt let herself out. "See you later."

She slammed the door, but not before she caught the hint of a smile on his face. It matched hers as she walked to the house.

Let him pretend that it was his job to warn her off. He'd returned for the same reason that she didn't want to leave. Home was home, whether that meant a place or person, or whether it took a day or half a lifetime to recognize that.

With every step, she could feel her spirit reviving. Cain was back.

It took Cain the rest of the afternoon to clear the debris from the barn and to divide it into what should be added to the existing brush pile in back and what could be recycled or used as kindling for a stove fire. After that, he stacked the new wood in the order that he would need it. By then it was time for Merritt to return to town.

"Hey!" he called, seeing she was already at the end of the driveway. Incredibly, she had one arm full of boxes and with the other she lugged the big tote. No telling what all she managed to get in there, he mused, seeing how it was almost dragging on the ground. "Wait up!"

She did pause and squinted at him. The sinking sun was in her eyes.

Hopping into the cab, Cain quickly turned the emptied truck around and drove down to her. This time, he got out and opened the door for her. Then he took the tote from her, grunting at its weight, while she situated the bakery boxes on the seat.

"No wonder I haven't seen so much as a glimpse of you getting firewood." Once she was done, he set the tote on the floorboard, then stood back as she situated herself between everything. "You've been busier than usual."

"Which is why I'm not burning as much firewood as usual," she told him. "Running the oven nonstop puts less work on the wood-burning stove. You wouldn't believe the cake and pie orders I have for Thanksgiving. All the more reason I'm grateful for the lift."

Her soft voice was a balm on his fractured soul and he yearned for the simple pleasure of listening to it all day—or better yet, all night. To keep from making a fool of himself, he shut the door, using the time it took to get back behind the wheel to get a grip on his emotions.

"No problem," he replied. "I'd gotten to a good stopping place. Couldn't very well start up on the roof when it's about to get dark. Thought I'd go for dinner."

"How long do you think it will take to get the hole sealed? I heard on Alvie's radio that the next storm might be blowing by the weekend."

"I've no idea. I've never done a repair job this big before."

"And the roof is steep."

"I've seen worse. I'll give it a good push tomorrow and that should give me a better idea. It's been a while since I've done any measuring or cutting, too. Good thing Leroy had an electric saw in the storage shed at the café or I'd be handsawing come March."

"I take it that heights don't bother you? Nah," she continued before he could answer. "Not a tough ex-marine."

Two points, Cain thought with admiration. She must have been itching for a chance to show him that she might not be able to control everything that happened around her, but she could try to understand it. "Okay," he drawled. "So you and Alvie discussed me."

"Leroy participated," Merritt offered helpfully.

"I'll bet he did." Cain flinched inwardly knowing the old buzzard wouldn't consider leaving out the barbershop buzz, which had to include his least respectable antics with certain ladies in the area.

"It's not his fault. It was just a natural progression," she told him. "After apologizing, Alvie said to tell you that you could do the roof. But by that time you were gone. I figured somewhere down the highway—or sitting in the backseat of a squad car for driving without a windshield and creating a traffic hazard. All Leroy did was try to explain how you were more resourceful than that."

Cain didn't believe a word of that. "I never made it as far as the interstate." He slid her a speaking glance. "I think I am smart enough to avoid blatant invitations to get arrested. On a hunch, I checked with the gas station mechanic here in town who restores old vehicles as a hobby. He was willing to work with me on payment for the windshield and door repairs. Long story short, that's where my salary for the roof is going."

"He does impressive work," Merritt said, as wide-eyed as a babe.

Cain shifted uncomfortably in his seat, mentally giving Leroy an earful. "After that was when I went to make peace with Alvie."

At the café, he was quick to assist her again and, this time, insisted on getting most of the boxes as well as the tote. "You get the door," he told her.

The place was empty, the dinner rush not yet started. They went straight into the back where Alvie was checking on entrées already in the oven. The scent of lasagna, pot roast and shrimp scampi pulled at Cain's stomach, reminding him that he'd skipped lunch.

"Cat's out of the bag about you being an angel and rescuing me with my truck repair," he murmured to Alvie, squeezing her shoulder.

"And they say women can't keep a secret," she pretended to scoff.

"Don't play innocent with me. Thanks to you and informative Leroy, I'm doing damage duty." But his mood was more wry than resentful. He wasn't one to blame the messengers. He could only try not to make himself fodder in the future.

While she'd undoubtedly heard everything, Merritt remained upbeat. "Have a seat whenever you want," Merritt told him. "I'll put together a breadbasket for you and get you started shortly."

With Leroy now upstairs for the night, Cain chose to sit at the end of the counter closer to the window, which was Merritt's side. He'd just finished reading the specials on one of the two blackboards on either end of the lunch counter when he heard the front door open. He glanced over his shoulder and saw Nikki breeze in.

As usual, she was dressed for style, not sense. At best, her short, red, faux-fur jacket warmed her arms and shoulder blades. Unzipped, it exposed that her green, deep V-necked sweater would let diners know that she was wearing a lacy push-up bra. Her black miniskirt advertised shapely, endless legs.

She broke stride upon noticing him, then smiled with sexual interest. Even though she was shacking up with Josh Bevans, the Paxton Ranch foreman, it didn't seem to stop her from testing her power on every other man who happened by.

"Hello, you," she said, circling around several tables to stroke the sleeve of his jean-jacket as though they were intimate friends. "Thought you left town?"

"Guess not."

She glanced around, causing her chandelier earrings to jingle. "Have you been waiting long? I'll fix you right up with silverware and—"

"Merritt knows I'm here. Thanks."

"You are welcome," she purred. "Anytime." As Merritt emerged from the back carrying silverware, a glass of water and a breadbasket, Nikki asked him loud enough for her to hear, "Where are you staying these days?" Then she giggled as she passed her.

Her expression carefully blank, Merritt reached him

and placed everything in its proper position. "She is the gift that keeps giving," she muttered.

He knew she was struggling not to expose her vulnerability, but he noticed her hands were not quite steady. Unable to resist, he reach across the counter and covered her hand with his to still her for a moment. "I don't know if *gift* is accurate. I suspect if we took a survey that word would be applied to you."

Although she looked flattered, she replied, "I'd better get your order in to Alvie. You must be seriously hungry if you're hallucinating."

With a much-maligned sigh, Cain withdrew his hand. "Make it the lasagna."

"It does smell good," she murmured.

"Sit down and have dinner with me before it gets crowded."

"Listen to you. You know full well that before things get too busy, I need to call the customers who ordered those pies and cakes to come get them."

He'd spoken without thinking, wanting only to spend some time with her. "Will you at least come by and let me feed you a bite or two? I know I'm sending you conflicting messages, but it's obvious that you've been burning calories you can't afford."

"That would send tongues wagging." Meeting his concerned gaze, she let down her guard for a second. "But thank you, Cain. That was beyond sweet."

As luck would have it, her area filled up quickly, so how or if she made those calls, he didn't know, although people did trickle in and leave with boxes. The diners kept her going without a break. They included a young family who said they were from Minnesota on their way to visit family in Seattle for Thanksgiving. Merritt was a big hit with their one-year-old son. The little package of energy giggled whenever she leaned over and intentionally let her braid swing before him. He grabbed at it repeatedly, chortling as she tickled him with the end. While Cain knew she was painfully shy with adults, he enjoyed seeing that she clearly adored kids. He ached to be that little boy and bury his face in the soft crook of her pale throat and shoulder.

Forcing himself to look away, he caught Nikki watching him. Uttering a curse under his breath, he reached for his wallet.

"No dessert?" Merritt asked, coming to take his plate and bring him his ticket.

"Too full. No change," he added, putting down a bill over the ticket. More quietly, he said, "Back to get you at closing."

"Only if it's convenient," she said with equal discretion. "Have a good evening," she added brightly for the sake of their audience. "Come back and see us."

The weather continued to cooperate, and by Wednesday when Merritt came home at midday, she saw that Cain had managed to close the gaping hole in the roof. But he'd done more than that. There was a smokestack to one side where one hadn't been before.

Curious to see how it looked inside—and too eager for any chance to spend a moment with him—she went to the barn and knocked on the door, despite both doors being wide open. She could see he was stooped over an old iron wood-burning stove placed on a brick base in the center of the barn.

"Now it can snow again," she said as her greeting. She was impressed with his progress as much as the quality of his work.

It would be good to have a way to warm the place that was practical. She had worried for him since she'd realized his intent was to sleep out here. After talking to Alvie, she'd gotten permission to borrow a long electrical cord that would reach the cottage, and an extra space heater. While appreciative of her boss and friend's generosity, Merritt believed that at least part of her kindness was triggered by the hope that this would keep Cain in the barn and out of the house.

"Hey, is it that time already?" Cain greeted her with a warm smile. "How did it go? Are you all done with the special orders?"

As busy as he was himself, he'd been making a point to ask how her work was going and to coax her to eat, to rest and to call him if she needed something repaired or retrieved from a high shelf or something. He was making all of the gestures of a man in a relationship, not just a friend. And yet, much to her frustration, gestures were all he was doing.

"The last one was picked up minutes before Alvie had designated the time we would lock up." She pumped the air, buoyed by adrenaline. "I can't believe I'm done until Christmas—or that we're off until Friday. Well, except to take care of us."

"Us?" An odd expression of uncertainty crossed his face. "You should spend the day pampering yourself, Merritt. You push yourself all the time."

"And what were you planning to do? Cain Paxton, don't be ridiculous. We're going to have our own celebration. Alvie and Leroy are coming, too." When he didn't immediately respond, she wondered if she'd made a mistake. "I should have asked you sooner. You have other plans, do you?"

"Yeah," he began slowly. "The old man invited me to join him at the ranch."

The words dripped with sarcasm, and yet Merritt found it easier to breathe again. "I wish that was true."

"I don't. I wouldn't go if it was."

Back in planning mode, Merritt said, "Make a request."

He raised his eyebrows. "For...?"

"Dinner. Dessert. We are going to celebrate. Isn't there *anything* you miss that you'd really like to have this Thanksgiving?"

"Mer, we never celebrated Thanksgiving."

"Well, now you are. You say you've been tortured by the scents emanating from the kitchen. Which one? Cinnamon, vanilla, pumpkin...pick something. If I don't have all of the ingredients for a recipe in the house, there's still time to go to the market."

"What would be easiest on you?"

She dropped her head back and growled at the bluest of skies. "Frustrating man. That does it." She shook her finger at him with mock fierceness. "I'm going to work and you can just hope for the best."

She was several feet away when she heard "Bet I'll get it, too."

Merritt didn't look back. She didn't want him to see how his tender words had brought tears to her eyes.

The next morning Merritt couldn't wait to scramble out of bed and begin the day. It was a good thing that she rose when she usually did because she lingered way too long on her appearance. Having done so well on her holiday orders, she'd allowed herself to splurge at the only boutique in town. It was the first time she *wanted* to. She had found a black skirt that gave the phrase "poetry in motion" new meaning. The way she figured, if she couldn't walk with grace, her outfit could at least make it seem as though she was. As for the white silk, long-sleeved blouse, she'd never owned anything so romantic in design. It had a raised lace collar, princess neckline and lace cuffs. Simple black suede slippers finished her ensemble.

She hardly recognized the young woman in the bathroom mirror. Continuing with her desire to look more her age, she brushed her hair for ten minutes, until it gleamed, before tying it over one shoulder with a strip of red satin ribbon. She'd been less indulgent on her makeup, allowing herself only a touch of rose lip gloss and a stroke or two of mascara; however, she thought the effects—enhanced by her excitement—were transforming.

She'd just put a Brahms cassette into the player, poured herself a first mug of coffee and tied on her apron when there was a knock at the back door. No doubt Cain had seen the lights on. The other day she'd told him that he should come over to shower or use the washer and dryer anytime. He had been—when she was at work. This time, he'd had no choice about timing.

"Whoa, who are you?" he said at the sight of her. He was carrying his change of clothes and almost stepped off the stoop in his surprise. "What did you do with Miller Moth?" he teased.

Merritt chuckled in delight as she stepped aside for him to enter. "Happy Thanksgiving. Make yourself at home. Do you want a mug of coffee to take in there with you?"

"That would be great. Merritt…you're lovely," he added, his voice lowered to a rasp.

She could only mouth her thanks; she didn't trust her voice, either. No one had ever used the word in relation to her, and it didn't matter if he was just being kind. She did feel pretty.

When he emerged in less than fifteen minutes, Cain was dressed in a rust-colored, suede Western shirt and new jeans. He'd polished his black Western boots, and even with his hair still wet, she'd never seen him look more handsome. His wound had healed to where he could skip the bandage, and the discoloration at his temple was hardly visible with his light bronze skin.

"Thank you," she said, suffering a moment of her old shyness. "I'm so glad you wanted to do this."

"In the service, one of the things some of the guys talked about most—despite the military preparing some pretty good spreads at the holidays—was their family gatherings. I have to admit I wanted to see what I was missing." After placing the bag with his other clothes on the washer to take home later, he gestured with his empty mug. "Is there still some left?"

"Coffee—help yourself. That goes for any of the treats or appetizers, as well. Alvie said they would be here by ten o'clock, so I waited on starting on a lot of the little things to make sure it's all fresh." First, though, she was putting the finishing touches on seasoning and stuffing the turkey.

As he moved around the counter to the coffeemaker, Cain looked over her shoulder. "Can I get that into the oven for you? That's a big bird."

"Bless you for asking." The turkey had started as a twenty-six-pounder, and with the stuffing and the roasting pan it had to be tipping thirty pounds since several scoops of dressing ago. She covered it with aluminum foil, which would come off in the last hour for browning, and opened the oven for him.

After he got his coffee, Cain asked for more to do, so she had him opening cans of olives and peeling hard-boiled eggs while she chopped celery, pickles, olives, peppers and ham for deviled eggs. Then he helped her move the kitchen table through the open doorway into the living room to give them more space.

Cain watched her bring out a borrowed tablecloth from Alvie and old china. "Now you're getting too fancy."

As she added wine goblets and a pair of candlesticks, she shook her head. "Alvie says the glasses are from a garage sale, and I picked up these candlesticks at the dollar store. Leroy said they were bringing wine, and a celebration isn't a celebration without candles."

"It's good to see you enjoying yourself—although it looks like an awful lot of work."

"Fun work. That's different."

About two hours later, as Cain was lighting the votive candles she had scattered around the cottage and the table ones, he called to her that Leroy's truck was pulling in. "You better come see what's catching a ride in the bed of the truck," he added.

Admittedly curious, Merritt emerged from the kitchen to join him as he opened the front door. She gasped in pleasure. "Oh, how wonderful—a tree!"

"I thought we needed something to do before and after dinner," Alvie called, beaming as she led the way inside. "Otherwise, Leroy will be suggesting poker." She was carrying a magnificent poinsettia plant that was as wide as it was tall, but her attention was all on Merritt. "Why, you look like you belong on the top of the tree, doesn't she, Leroy?"

He followed bearing a small mountain of boxes, clearly lights and ornaments. "Nothing wrong with a friendly game of poker." He stopped to kiss Merritt's cheek. "Where've you been hiding yourself, sweet thing?"

While Alvie set her plant on the table by the streetside window, Leroy yielded his teetering load to the chair nearest the front door. Heaving a sigh, he motioned to Cain. "You want to help me with the tree? Alvie had to have the biggest one in the lot."

"If I'd wanted a dusting wand, I would've brought the one that comes with the vacuum cleaner," Alvie replied. "This is our first tree in I can't remember how many years," she added to Merritt. "You don't mind us going overboard, do you, honey?"

Merritt knew exactly how long it had been, but merely grinned. "Bring it on."

They set the eight-foot spruce by the window to the right of the door to get it as far as possible from the drying effects of the stove. Alvie had already arranged for the stand to be put on it and said all it needed now was water. Cain went for that while Alvie shed her black quilted jacket, exposing her white sweatshirt over black sweatpants and red elf slippers with bells on the tips. She thrust out her ample chest to draw attention to the embossed cardinal and the rhinestone-adorned snowflakes.

"I'm the spirit of Christmas coming. Happy Thanksgiving, sweet girl. Thank you for doing this."

She inspected each bowl and serving dish, clucked over how big and juicy the turkey looked and moaned in pleasure over the way the house smelled. "Good enough to lick the walls," she said and spun around to yell to Leroy, "Music! Where's that radio?"

Posted at the stove to warm his backside, Leroy looked pained. He had just removed his jacket and was only in his usual uniform of white shirt and jeans. "In the truck next to the wine. I'll get it in a second. Let me defrost from my last trip out. You've got music," he added, referring to the cassette playing.

"And it's nice—for a memorial service." Her hazel eyes began to twinkle with mischievousness. "I'm ready to boogie."

Leroy replied, "And I can feel my Arthur getting ready to make a speech."

Merritt knew he was referring to his own arthritis, which he said that he'd lived with longer than he had Alvie, so it deserved its own name. She sent Cain a look of appeal.

"I'll go." Cain dashed outside without even pausing to put on his jacket.

Alvie tilted her head to watch him through the

window. "I have to say he cleans up well," she told Merritt. "Look at him risking pneumonia to show off for a pretty woman."

As she felt herself blush, Merritt drew her attention to the table. "What do you think? Cain was worried that things were getting too formal when I brought out the wineglasses and candles."

"Poor guy probably has the first instinct to reject anything that might make him seem even remotely like his grandfather. It's jug wine. Screw top, no cork. Cheap and sweet is my motto and I have the figure to prove it." She started. "Leroy, call to him to get the wine, too. It's in the bag behind the passenger seat."

Soon the house was even more festive as carols played softly in between top country-western tunes. Alvie drafted Cain to pour from the fat jug. When the four of them had their glasses in hand, she raised hers.

"To good company," she said, almost immediately getting emotional.

"Absolutely," Merritt murmured as Leroy patted Alvie's back.

"The best," Cain said, his eyes on Merritt.

After everyone touched glasses, they sipped. Alvie declared, "Let's party!"

Merritt encouraged them to nibble on the appetizers and Leroy talked Cain into testing the lights before they removed them from the boxes. There was laughter and fussing, and Leroy decided that since Cain was taller, he should be in charge of stringing the upper branches of the tree.

"I'll just stand here and supervise," he added from

the stove, glass in hand. In between directives, he sang a line from whatever song was playing at the moment.

It was just past noon when Merritt announced the turkey was done. As she picked up the platter from the center of the table to bring it into the kitchen, Cain abandoned the tree work.

"Let me." He grasped her by the waist before she could reach for the oven door.

It was pitiful that such a benign touch should send her heart into palpitations, but it did. Merritt was grateful that Alvie was too busy collecting everyone's glasses to bring them to the table to notice her self-conscious state.

When they sat down, Alvie took over again to say grace. Merritt didn't mind a bit. She liked that Alvie finally felt comfortable here again.

"Thank you, Lord," Alvie began, "for this table and continued good company. Amen."

Leroy mused, "You've gotta quit being such a wind-bag."

"He's busy today. He appreciates us not tying up the lines. Are you going to carve or make Cain think I just keep you around as my sex toy?"

Everyone laughed and, with chest high, Leroy stood to carve. The side dishes were passed around—sweet potatoes, grilled vegetables, spinach soufflé, sweet baby carrots and both corn bread stuffing and a richer one with sausage, dates, apples and wild rice. Merritt had made her own cranberry sauce from scratch, and she was testing a new cracked-wheat-and-nut dinner roll.

The raves were plentiful until she shushed them. "I

don't believe a word of it. If you were really pleased, you'd be stuffing your mouths, not talking."

And that's what they did for a good while—at least through "I'll Be Home For Christmas" and Taylor Swift's catchy Romeo and Juliet warble. Cain was the one to set down his fork and reach for his wineglass. "To our chef and hostess. I can honestly say that I've never had an experience like this before."

Merritt could no more try to keep her glass in her hand than meet anyone's eyes. She hid behind her linen napkin and begged them to stop. "You're going to make me cry."

"Me, too," Alvie said, sniffing.

"I'd three it, but I can't," Leroy piped in, "because I don't want to walk home tonight. But, Merritt, honey—" When she did look up, he pointed his forked two fingers at his eyes and then directed them at her.

They all laughed again.

After another minute, Merritt asked Leroy, "Didn't your kids want to come back for a visit?"

"They keep talking about it. Unlike so many, they can afford it, but they have too many commitments and too little time," he said. "It would be easier if I went to one coast and then the other, but it would take a court order and a crowbar to get me to fly. Besides, despite this hot physique—" he smoothed his hands over his skinny chest "—I am too modest to be exposed by those newfangled radar machines. Maybe when we retire, Alvie and I will rent a car and take a road trip."

"Can you imagine? The two of us, who have never driven farther than Helena, trying to navigate around the country?" Alvie giggled. "If you ever get a call asking you to accept charges from Guatemala, do it. It's us. Lost."

Although she grinned, Merritt knew she was half-serious. Whenever a diner from out of town called needing directions, Alvie always called on her. "They have GPS devices now that will talk you through every turn. Or you could take a bus like I did. And there's always trains."

Leroy brightened. "A train would be romantic." He leaned close to squeeze Alvie's hand.

Merritt inhaled with pleasure. "The house is beginning to pick up the scent of the tree. I just love that."

"Me, too," Alvie said. "I'm having second thoughts about the ornaments, though. They're just this and that. Stuff I saved over the years, even from my own childhood. Come to think of it, they may be too chipped and ratty-looking to use. Don't be kind because you think you'll hurt my feelings. There's nothing wrong with a half-decorated tree while you wait to buy your own things."

"Oh, no," Merritt assured her. "I can't wait to see them and hear you tell us their history. Our last tree was plastic—or cellophane—supposedly white, but it was about as white as New York City snow. My mother bought a can of paint and thought she would spray it green, but some wise guys had changed the caps and we had a fluorescent orange tree. She bought a box of candy canes for a dollar and those were the ornaments. By Christmas there weren't any more ornaments on the tree. We'd eaten them when there wasn't enough food."

"Sounds as much fun as on the reservation," Cain said. "Except we didn't have any tree."

They decided they would work off some of the meal before tackling dessert, so the men went to finish stringing the lights, while Merritt and Alvie cleaned off the table a bit.

"Just put everything in the sink," Merritt told her once they had carried in the first load of dirty dishes. "I'll take care of them later."

"Nonsense." Alvie checked the cabinet under the sink and brought out the large washbowl and filled it with hot water and soap. "We have to give the guys a minute to get on a roll again before we can point out how they're not doing it right." She laughed lustily at her own humor.

Shaking her head, Merritt headed back to the table. "You're all bark and no bite."

When she had the food wrapped and set on the counter for later nibbling, she began drying the things Alvie had in the drainer. "I don't think there's going to be anything to tease them about. They're doing a great job."

"Cain's trying hard to please you."

"Oh, Alvie…"

"What? Whenever he thinks no one is paying attention, he's eating you up with his eyes."

While that thrilled her to no end, she didn't want to encourage her. "I thought you had reservations about him?"

"Honey, I have reservations about *Leroy.* But I do have enough female DNA to always hope for a happy ending." Alvie finished with the washing for now, dried her hands and touched Merritt's cheek. "Angel, I know you had a rough childhood yourself. I may need reading glasses more than I wear them, but there's nothing wrong with my other kind of vision. You need a hero. I hope he's it."

They returned to the living room as Cain and Leroy were standing back to gauge the success of their efforts. Cain thought some lights needed moving. Leroy thought ornaments would hide all flaws.

"Those tiny white bulbs sparkle like stars," Alvie all but cooed.

"It's going to look absolutely gorgeous at night," Merritt added.

Holding his near-empty glass, Leroy began swaying to the music. "Recognize this one, Alvie?" Grinning, he sidled over to her, wrapped his free hand around her ample waist and began to dance with her.

Alvie transformed into a young woman again and touched her cheek against his. "Our song."

Actually, it was a new rendition of an oldie and Merritt came to slip the glass from Leroy's fingers. "So you can hold her properly," she murmured. She set it on his place at the table. Fred and Ginger they weren't; nevertheless, she sighed wistfully at their obvious pleasure in each other.

"I don't have much experience with that," Cain said near her ear. "But I can shuffle."

Just having his hands on her waist again almost turned her into a stuttering fool. "I've never even done that much."

He looked down at her small feet. "I don't think you can hurt me. The trick will be not to hurt you." The words were playful; the expression in his eyes as he turned her to face him was anything but.

"Don't warn me off. Not today."

She barely moved her lips on the words that were quickly whispered. She really didn't expect him to hear them, but incredibly he gave up and drew her into his arms.

Merritt heard him whisper "Damn it" near her temple, and she closed her eyes, willing him to accept this feeling. She was. The slow, romantic tune was about longing, and he rocked her gently, until she stopped thinking and simply let herself be caught up in the web of magic the day was weaving around them.

"Will you get a load of them?" Leroy said from behind Cain. "They don't even hear that the song is over."

A low rumble rose in Cain's throat, but he did stop. After touching his lips to Merritt's forehead, he released her.

She stepped around him and said brightly, "Let's get the ornaments hung."

For the next half hour or so, she and Alvie did that, while the men had another glass of wine and offered a running commentary about the effects in between forays into local politics and who was likely to win the football games that neither of them were interested in watching.

Merritt was enchanted with the decorations, particularly the mercury-glass pieces and the birds with feather tails. "They've held up well," she told Alvie.

"The wrapping sure hasn't." Alvie shook her head at the tired tissue paper and mildewed cardboard boxes. "When you take all this down, you might want to replace everything, maybe invest in a couple of plastic storage containers before you put it up. Then again, you could just toss everything and start your own collection."

"Throw away memories like these? No way!" Merritt couldn't believe she'd suggested such a thing. "I will get the containers. Are you sure you want me to keep them here?"

Alvie shrugged. "It's not like I'm going to put up another tree. I'd rather you invite us here."

Merritt held up a dainty glass bird with a clip base as the feet. "I'm going to get a chair and put this one on one of the short branches near the top."

"I heard that," Cain said, coming up behind her. Grasping her by the waist, he said, "Get ready." Then he lifted her up and held her as she fastened the ornament.

"Got it."

"Worried that I'd drop you?" he drawled as he set her back on the hardwood floor. "If anything, I'd be more concerned about snapping those finch bones of yours."

Maybe, but for a man who didn't want anything to do with her, he was quick to come to her aid. "I may be small, but I'm durable," she said with a lift of her chin.

"Good, then get another ornament that you think will fit up there and let's get that part over with. I don't want you to get any ideas about finishing this later."

As Leroy grasped Alvie's hands for a slow swing to the next song, Merritt did as Cain directed and pointed to the branch she intended it for.

When she was down on the floor again, she mused, "You're as handy as a cherry picker." Next she chose a delicate, frosted-glass pear and pointed again, but this time the branch was facing the window. "There, please. Is that too difficult? Maybe if I get a chair you should do it."

"Oh, ye of little faith." Cain set her onto his right shoulder. "Now balance yourself by holding my hand." He kept her in place by wrapping his right arm around her thighs, then he inched between the tree and the window. "Okay?"

"Almost. A little more." She still had to stretch to reach the branch. "Oh—stop shaking."

"You're the one shaking." He laughed.

"I'm slipping—"

With an incredible show of strength and agility, Cain flipped her as she came down to keep her from going into the window, only that brought her body intimately against his. The material of her wispy skirt clung to his shirt and her bare legs stroked against his groin and thighs. Even that was nothing compared to finding herself eye-to-eye, nose-to-nose, mouth-to-mouth with him for breathless seconds.

She watched fire light in his dark eyes and his body grow even tighter as his gaze dropped to her mouth. Just as she parted her lips to welcome him, she heard Alvie.

"Oh, that was fun. I'm ready for dessert."

It was a relief to see that they were hidden by the tree. Cain must have realized that, too, because as he eased her the rest of the way to the floor, he made no attempt to protect her from his arousal.

"I—" She brushed at her wayward skirt and smoothed her hair. "I'll get the coffeemaker going."

How she managed to make it to the kitchen on her

weak legs, she didn't know, but she was grateful that the desserts seemed to be what captivated Alvie and Leroy. When they sat down to a selection of pies, cakes, pastries and cookies that Merritt had created, a still-subdued Cain first asked for a slice of the pumpkin. Leroy wanted pecan and Alvie was intrigued with the chocolate-glazed torte with the crushed peppermint candies as decoration.

"You have to bring the rest of this to the café tomorrow," she said. "I think you've created something that'll be a big hit. Is that mint liqueur in there?"

"Just a touch of crème de cacao. It's the cracked candies that make you think it's the other liqueur."

"I have to try that," Leroy and Cain said at the same time.

It was dusk when Alvie yawned and said, "You'd better get us home, Leroy. I need my beauty sleep if I'm supposed to smile at bacon at six tomorrow morning."

As they collected their things and headed for the door, she hugged Merritt. "We had such a grand time. Thank you, dearest."

"Me, too," Merritt assured her. "See you in the morning."

As they pulled away, Cain went out to get enough wood to keep the stove going through the night.

"Would you like another cup of coffee or wine?" she asked when he was done. Alvie had insisted they leave the wine here.

"That wouldn't be a good idea," Cain replied, looking at the floor. Finally he looked at her. "You need the words? You're a temptation, I admit it. But I'm leaving while I still have the discipline to behave myself."

Merritt followed him to the back door as though he was a magnet. "What if I said you don't need to?"

Cain turned around and with the back of his fingers caressed the hair cascading over her shoulder and breast. Merritt's heart leapt against the knuckles that were sensitizing her nipple.

"I'd say that would be a bigger mistake because this isn't all I'd want to do with you."

"Kiss me," she whispered. "I know it won't mean anything more to you, but I want to know what a real kiss feels like."

"I don't want to be part of an experiment."

Stung, she began to turn away. He caught her and lifted her off her feet and against him. Then he claimed her mouth with his, making a mockery of his words, and began a sensual assault.

Merritt wrapped her arms around him and kissed him back to the best of her ability.

With a groan Cain held her even tighter, his kiss growing more hungry. "Do you feel it?" he asked.

"You're angry with me."

"No. I'm starving for a woman and I couldn't be gentle."

"I don't believe you. And I'm not afraid. Not of you."

With a groan, Cain set her down and muttered, "Well, I am of you." Then he brushed past her and let himself out the back door.

Chapter Six

It wouldn't have surprised Merritt if Cain had left that night, but he didn't. He did, however, keep his distance for several days after that. She would see smoke rising from the barn stack, and at night saw light on in there, since he continued to use the extension cord, though not the heater. From what little she gleaned from conversations between Alvie and Leroy, Cain had asked to rent the place because he'd gotten a few handyman jobs in the area. Alvie wouldn't take any money. She justified herself by claiming that she owed him because his presence scared away troublemakers and she slept better knowing Merritt wasn't completely alone.

It was a surprise to have him knock on the back door one afternoon only minutes before she was due to leave for the café's evening shift. When she paused in packing her insulated tote to open the back door, she met his frowning countenance with curiosity.

"I'll be right there," she said, thinking he resented that driving her into town was a given now. "I was just packing up."

He hooked his thumb over his shoulder. "I came over to tell you to just take the truck. The keys are in it. I'm trying to finish a cabinet."

"I can walk."

"It's going to snow again tonight. Don't be stubborn, Merritt."

She could have said something about that, but she merely reminded him, "I don't have an up-to-date license." Even though they hardly spoke, Merritt was grateful that he continued to drive her to work daily and pick her up.

"Nobody's going to bother you. See you later."

There was no reason to not believe that he was busy—Merritt often heard him hammering or sawing away at something in the barn—but she was still disappointed. Nevertheless, she packed up and eased down the road. She wasn't nervous, the old truck handled like a tank and she certainly didn't go over the speed limit.

The shift at the restaurant was no improvement over how things were going with Cain. A pair of wise-guy customers from the Paxton Ranch, who sat in Nikki's area, kept acting up, trying to get her frazzled, and Nikki mostly let them get away with it. Merritt guessed that the redhead wasn't happy that she had started to dress nicer and was wearing a little makeup. On top of that, during the young men's antics, Nikki didn't hesitate in being especially attentive to Merritt's customers to suggest that Merritt wasn't doing her job.

"Imagine me the object of jealousy," Merritt said to

Alvie after they'd closed up and Nikki made her usual fast getaway.

"Told you, Miller Moth." Alvie slid her a tired but wicked look. "A little moth has no trouble being graceful and magical compared to a stinkbug."

Merritt tried and failed to repress a laugh. "That is an awful analogy."

"Not when that selfish bit of trash tries to mess with my business, which I'm sure slipped past the vacancy sign in her mind."

Alvie had a point, Merritt thought as she walked to the truck. People wanted to be able to eat in a peaceful atmosphere. Employee conflict wasn't conducive to that. At least she hadn't had to deal with Sanford's unwelcome attention in the last few days. That would have been one dose of stress too much.

It had begun to snow about an hour ago, and a few inches were already turning the streets white again. She slid as she neared the truck, but managed to grab the door's handle to steady herself. It was a relief to climb inside and escape the wind, then to hear the engine crank to life with minimal coaxing. Her plan was to get a batch of biscuit dough into the fridge for tomorrow's biscuits, and then she intended to make it an early night. This weather system was getting to her tonight, too.

Right after she turned toward home, lights appeared in the rearview mirror. Keeping her eyes on the road, she reached up to tilt the mirror so the beams wouldn't blind her. In these conditions, she wasn't going to accelerate for anyone. The driver could go ahead and pass her if he was so eager to risk his safety. As soon as she made the curve, she flipped on her right blinker to indicate she was getting off the road shortly.

The vehicle in back did speed up then and start to pass, only to cut into her side too soon. Merritt gasped, "Fool—watch out!"

She had to jerk the steering wheel sharply to the right to avoid a collision. That shot her off the road. Not thinking, she hit the brakes, which slid her into the ditch and snow and cost her tire traction. Acting like it had a life of its own, the truck climbed the other side of the embankment in a direct line toward the big old oak she generally loved to pass under on her daily commutes.

Convinced a collision was imminent, she was flung forward and she screamed, then struck the large, old-fashioned steering wheel.

"Ow!"

The sharp pain blinded her momentarily, quickly replaced by the lesson that the stereotype about seeing stars was actually a truth. But what on earth— She hadn't hit the tree? Roots, she realized. The big protruding roots must have stopped her. Dazed but relieved she pressed her fingers to the piercing throbbing. There was no blood yet, but it didn't feel like part of her head.

"Merritt!"

She heard his voice about the same time that the door was yanked open. Along with wind and blowing snow, Cain leaned in. Merritt had never been happier to see him.

"Are you hurt?"

"I'm so sorry. But I didn't hit the tree. How did you get up here?"

"You're running a little late, so I came out to see if maybe the truck wasn't acting right for you."

"It was that other truck that didn't cooperate." As things became clearer, she realized something. "He intentionally cut me off. What a couple of idiots."

"I didn't recognize the vehicle," Cain said, glancing over his shoulder in the direction the vehicle had gone. "Of course, he kept going and the snow was too intense to get a look at the license plate. Wait—you said idiots. There were two in the truck?"

"Yeah."

"Damn fools probably recognized the truck as mine and thought on a night like this they could get away with harassing me."

"No, they knew I was driving," she countered. "They're friends of Nikki's. Sort of. They work for her boyfriend at the ranch and had dinner at the café this evening. I have to admit their behavior wasn't much better there, so I shouldn't be surprised this happened."

As soon as she saw Cain's expression, she regretted sharing that. "They're overgrown kids with too much time on their hands."

"Put this thing in Reverse and I'll push. I'm taking you back into town to report this to the police."

Merritt knew that with a knot growing on her forehead, she had an excuse to make a rash decision, but he was the one who wasn't thinking clearly. She grabbed the sleeve of his jacket as he started for the front of the truck. "You don't need to go anywhere near the police station in the mood you're in. There's no real harm done. Besides, I'm outside the city limits."

"I don't care. No deputy is coming out here tonight unless someone with power demands they do."

As he firmly shut the door, Merritt shivered. She had such a bad feeling about this.

For the first time, she regretted his strength. He had minimal trouble getting her over the protruding roots and within a minute or two, she was back on the road, but she intentionally turned the truck so that it was facing toward home.

Cain returned to the driver's side and opened the door. "Slide over." Once inside, he said, "Let me see your forehead." He had to move her hand, and when he did he winced. "That must throb, but at least the skin's not broken."

"It does. An ice pack and aspirin would help a lot more than what you have in mind. Hint, hint."

Instead, he cut a U-turn.

She wasn't happy. "Why can't we go home? I'm exhausted and want to go to bed. As it is, I'll have to get up earlier to make the biscuits that I'm not preparing the dough for now."

He ignored her and drove back to town and parked in front of the police station. When Merritt tried to exit via the passenger side, he took hold of her by the wrist and swept her out on his side. Then he carried her until they were under the awning on dry sidewalk.

She might have enjoyed that if they weren't on a head-on collision with trouble.

A lone officer was on duty. Thankfully, it wasn't Jerry Posner. Maybe he'd come down with the flu or, better yet, she thought, quit? Merritt knew the pale, curly-haired man as the reserve officer, Toby Booker, who filled in if someone was on vacation or sick.

"Help you folks?"

Since he didn't appear to know Cain, Merritt quickly said, "Hi, Booker. I'm Merritt Miller." She pointed with her thumb over her shoulder. "I'm a waitress across the street? A couple of guys drove me off the road just now. Cain thinks I need to show you this." She brushed away wayward tendrils to give him a better view of the lump forming just above her left eyebrow.

"Wow. Yeah, that's a good one. Where exactly did it happen? I didn't hear anything."

Merritt gave Cain a "told you" glance. "Yeah, well… it was almost by Alvie Crisp's house around the bend."

"Right, you're the one living there now." He actually looked relieved. "You know that's not our jurisdiction. You really should talk to the sheriff's office. Want me to get them on the phone for you?"

"No."

"Yes."

Merritt gave Cain a pleading look. "I don't have a license," she reminded him under her breath.

Cain exhaled with exasperation and looked back at the younger man. "No one is coming in this weather and you know it. Look, make sure Chief Robbins knows about what she said happened when he comes in tomorrow morning. Have him inform Sanford Paxton that his clowns might have gotten away with things last time, but if Merritt so much as suffers a broken nail because of their recklessness in the future, they'll have to answer to me."

Cain's restraint must have given Toby courage because he sat up straighter and thrust out his chest. "Now see here, you can't go making threats."

"I'm not. I'm making a promise." With that Cain ushered Merritt out of there.

"Nice," she said as he helped her get back into the truck. "That should guarantee a visit by the sheriff in the morning." She didn't think it was possible, but her head was beginning to hurt even more.

Cain scooped up a handful of snow and formed it into a flat pack, which he held to what was now a golf ball–size lump. "You may be used to people beating you down, but I'm not and never will be."

"And how has that worked for you?"

He looked like he was about to do something, then he leaned back in the seat and closed his eyes. "I'm not trying to be a hardnose, Mer. It was seeing you drive off the road. That tree blocked my view for a second and I didn't know if you—"

As he bit off the rest of what he'd intended to say and turned away, Merritt lowered the pack of snow in order to study his profile. What she saw had her leaning her head on his shoulder and stroking his arm. This had to be reminding him of his uncle, and who knew who else?

"I should never have let you drive alone," he continued. "What was I thinking?"

"It's over, and nothing serious happened."

"If Sanford doesn't contact you tomorrow to apologize and assure you that steps have been taken, I'm going to the ranch."

"In that case, I hope it snows three feet tonight." If necessary, she could let the air out of his tires…pull the distributor cap out from under the hood—if she remembered which one that was.

His silence the rest of the way home added to her unease. She knew better than to hope that he wouldn't follow her into the house. She made a far better nurse than patient. Convinced that she looked like a space creature growing a new eyeball in the middle of her forehead, all she wanted to do was crawl into bed and pull a blanket over her head.

As though reading her mind, once they were inside, he said, "Let me see that bump in this brighter light. I have to check your eyes, too."

"Dilation. Got it," she said wearily.

He'd parked right at the back door, so they'd entered into the kitchen, where the fluorescent lights did nothing for her appearance on a good day. Fatalistically, she stopped in the middle of the room and, hugging herself, looked upward at the overhead fixture. *Might as well get it over with,* she thought. The good news was that he would be so turned off that he would hightail it to the barn soon enough.

In a classic case of contradiction, he instantly transformed into being all tenderness and protective. "Ah, Mer. Sorry for the cold hands." He gently framed her face and turned her head from side to side to inspect her. "The good news is that you missed a concussion yourself, and the need for stitches. The bad news is that I was still luckier—you're going to have a brutal shiner by morning."

She could just imagine the looks she'd be getting at the café. But she quipped, "Hey, sympathy tips."

"Merritt, don't joke."

Giving up, she dropped her arms and all pretense. "Don't joke, don't argue, don't look at you, don't do this, don't do that…you know what would be easier, Cain? Just tell me what I'm allowed to do because I'm tired of failing."

As she started to step around him hoping to flee to the bedroom, he swept her into his arms. "You aren't failing," he said, tucking her head under his chin. "You're succeeding, too well."

Did she just hear what she thought she did? Feeling as dazed as she had after the crash, Merritt gently pushed against his chest so she could lean back and see his face. "Who knew?"

He shook from a silent chuckle, then groaned, starting to turn away. "This is such a bad idea…you're hurt."

This time she stopped him by grasping the front of his jacket with both hands. "I'm *fine*."

"And I can't do this anymore. I want you too much." Cain touched his lips to her injury, then he slowly took her mouth with his. His lips were firm, warm and quickly hungry.

Merritt kissed him back the same way he was teaching her, afraid that he would change his mind. When he sought the inner depths of her mouth, she let him have it. Freezing only seconds ago, she was suddenly warm, heading for hot, and she resented her jacket, his and the rest of the clothes that were keeping them apart. Fortunately, he seemed to settle the battle going on in his mind and carried her to the bedroom, leaving the door open so that there was only the light from the other side of the house filtering in. Setting her on her feet, he began unfastening her jacket.

His jacket was never buttoned, so Merritt just pushed it off his shoulders, until he shrugged out of it to let it fall to the floor where he then dropped hers.

"Pretty," he murmured, taking in her powder-blue cardigan sweater. But then he sighed over the tiny buttons. "My hands are too big not to damage those."

She did it for him, leaving him to crouch and remove her boots. When he directed her to sit, she did and stroked the head bowed studiously over his task. Yes, his hands weren't built for tiny things, she mused, but he was careful in his haste.

Once he had her bared of boots and socks, he sat beside her and tugged off his. He noted her quiet study and smiled. "These moments might feel awkward for you."

"No."

Clearly not believing her, he explained, "There's no choreography to make it romantic."

"I could watch you reading the paper and not be bored."

"While I," he said, slipping her sweater off her shoulders, "am going nuts thinking about how often I've wanted to do this." Gazing at the fair skin he exposed, he sighed. "Dear God, you have incredible skin."

Bending his head, he brushed his lips across her shoulder and along her throat. At the same time, he stroked her arms and then her back.

Merritt knew he was getting her used to his touch,

but she didn't tell him that she already was. She liked his petting *too* much.

He urged her hands to his shirt and she obediently plucked open the snaps on his black-and-white flannel shirt. Not needing more encouragement, she reached inside to explore his bronze, hairless chest. He looked and felt as smooth and hard as a piece of sculpture.

Cain's breath came like wind rustling autumn leaves. "I go to sleep imagining your lips on me. Do you want mine on you?"

To answer him, she eased down onto the quilt-style bedspread, then reached behind her to unfasten her plain, cotton bra. But the expression on his face soon had her pausing. "What?"

"Your trust. I'm cherishing it."

His kiss was worshipping as he eased the straps down her arms and caressed all of her with the material as he slid it off her. He replaced it with his hands and his mouth, which soon had her burying her hands in his hair and bowing off the bed.

"That's the way it's supposed to feel," he whispered against her skin. "And like this…"

He traced a series of kisses down her slim body while going to work removing her jeans and panties. When her damaged hip was exposed, he lingered there and his caresses were as soothing as any balm she'd tried for relief.

"Some of the worst wounds are invisible," he murmured.

"But don't treat me like I'll break."

"Easy for you to say. You're like a sleek handful of

porcelain." Even so, he eased his hand between her thighs. "Is this part new?"

His gaze held hers. She couldn't have lied if she wanted to—and she did because she was afraid he would stop. "Yes."

His eyelids grew heavy and his eyes darkened with desire. "I'd hoped otherwise. Then again, I wanted you to be. I couldn't stand thinking of him or anyone not making your first time right."

As he probed deeper, Merritt gripped the bedding, then his strong arms, unable to keep from moving against the covers, unable to resist him as he spread her legs wider.

"You're as honest as you are hungry. Do you know how arousing that is?"

When he replaced his fingers with his mouth, she gasped as she was propelled into a previously unknown consciousness. She closed her eyes, giving herself to it, to him, and cried out at her first taste of intimate pleasure. Until now, her awareness of nerve endings had been attributed to pain. She couldn't believe those same tiny sensors could bring her this wholly different reality.

Before she could peak again, he lured her back, then shifted to unzip his jeans.

Her entire being abuzz with intoxicating sensations, Merritt used the opportunity to explore him more. She was awed by his strength and size, amazed that he controlled his body with surprising grace and agility. She noticed that his nipples were as hard as hers, and she awarded the same kind of caresses to them that he'd shown her, enjoying that she had the power to make his breath catch and hiss.

As he dug into a pocket before kicking the jeans in the direction of the rest of their things, she looked at the foil packet in his hand. "Was I supposed to have that?" she asked.

"Hell, no."

She took no offense at his guttural growl, nor his predatory look. "Do I put it on you?"

He went from impassioned to tortured in a matter of heartbeats. "Merri...jeez."

When he bowed his head, as though in pain, she wondered. What had she done wrong?

Taking a deep breath, Cain slid the condom on. "Next time," he said, coming closer to caress her thigh with his arousal. Lowering his head, he wet her left breast with his mouth and teased her with his tongue and teeth, then repeated that on the other. Probing between her thighs, he continued, "Next time, we're going to do everything to each other. As much as we want. For as long as we can last."

His voice was dark suede, warming and seductive as he eased himself into her. The sensual invasion left Merritt feeling stretched and filled beyond what she thought possible. Her entire being demanded participation and she instinctively wrapped herself around him, innocent to the reality of how that just brought him deeper faster.

"Easy," he coaxed.

She obeyed because it suddenly felt as though a dagger was about to impale her from her womb to her heart. But then, thanks to Cain's tender ministrations, slowly, by increments, he made her trust that it was safe to breathe normally again.

"It gets better from here on, sweetness," he rasped between encouraging kisses and strokes.

Like a newborn seeking nourishment, she sought and captured his mouth, and with a deep-throated groan, he let her experience his barely tethered restraint. The passion and pleasure that she'd felt earlier turned out to be a shadow of the promise building. Soon his gentle rocking evolved into stronger, steady thrusts, and the effects of that piercing sweetness was almost too much to bear.

"Help me." Her voice sounded like a keening to her own ears. She wasn't strong enough, she understood now, and didn't want to disappoint him. He would try to stop out of concern, she just knew it. "Cain."

After only a slight hesitation, he locked his mouth to hers as he changed the rhythm of his thrusts and intensified them. His tongue drove into her with equal passion. Merritt felt something impossible, something like a wave lift and carry her. Behind her closed lids, the universe turned gold, then white. She thought she was being torn apart, yet simultaneously being born. And then the wave pushed her over and through and a helpless sob broke from her tight throat.

Almost immediately, Cain went rigid; then, with a deep shudder, he collapsed against her, his face buried in the curve of her neck and shoulder.

You should be drop-kicked from here to the Pacific.
Still pulsating from his climax, Cain forced himself to his elbows to give her relief from his weight. No

small feat, when all he wanted to do was soak in every delicious ounce of her any and every way imaginable. Guilt followed with excruciating speed. Despite trying to be as careful as possible, her pelvis and hip had to be killing her. Yet she was lying still and peaceful, as though in the deepest sleep.

Of course she was exhausted. She'd *started* exhausted, had been even before the damned accident. While he—he cursed himself anew as his body stirred to life within her.

He'd intended to go to another town, up to Billings or Helena once he'd given up on cold showers and masturbation ebbing his hunger. But he hadn't been able to make himself do it. It wasn't just sex he craved; he wanted what made sex better. Best. As a result, he hadn't been able to leave her alone.

Had he ruined the precious whatever that existed between them? He needed to know. He had to see the honesty that her words might try to hide.

"Look at me."

As still as she was, he knew she wasn't asleep. When she looked at him with those soul-grabbing dark eyes, he saw a woman aware. The innocence of the virgin was gone. And yet her pureness remained. Overwhelmed with gratitude, he took her hand and lifted it to his lips.

"How bad was it?" he forced himself to ask.

She blinked, a slight frown shadowing her eyes. "I wouldn't use that word. But…there were so many incredibly good feelings." She took his hand and placed it low on her abdomen. "Such need. Do you get that?"

"I get that," he said gruffly." He shook his head.

"That's what made me selfish. I should have tended to this first," he said, touching his lips to her bruise. "I should have waited one more day. That's proof of how easily you get under my skin."

A subtle, wicked pleasure lit in her eyes. "I like knowing that. I also like how you can't hide it from me anymore. I mean physically. It's going to be hard now to first look into your eyes and not at your jeans when we're in public."

His chest shook again suppressed laughter, but he was only minimally kidding when he growled, "Just make sure I'm the only guy you do that to."

Heaven help him, he was falling for her, and hard. As a man who had never been in love before, that wasn't an entirely comfortable feeling. She was too young—not chronologically, but life-wise. Perhaps most troubling was that she was too decent and noble. She'd already had a life of hard work with little to show for it. That's all she could look forward to with him. He had no real education, and *did* have a couple of serious black marks against him. What did he have to offer her but his heart and commitment?

If life was a baseball game, he would be in the bottom of the ninth inning with two strikes against him. That was nothing to bet on.

Merritt stroked her finger along the faint scar on his chin. "Are you finally going to tell me how you got this one?"

"I fell off a mountain."

She looked started. "Seriously?"

"Literally. I hated school, so I would go up into the foothills with my little twenty-two rifle and my horse.

I was trying to prove to myself that I could live up there on my own. On that particular trip, I came upon a rattlesnake sunning itself on a ledge I had to get by to continue and my horse spooked. I rolled and dropped about twenty feet. I was lucky the only damage was a broken nose, this scar and a long walk home."

"I'd have been terrified that the snake would come down after me."

"He became eagle dinner. That's why I didn't see the snake sooner. I was focusing on a family of the birds teaching their young to hunt."

"You weren't afraid having to walk down by yourself?"

"I was reasonably concerned since my rifle was still on the horse, but afraid? No. I still had a good knife, I knew where I was and my horse waited for me halfway down the trail. It was a good day."

"Your poor grandmother must have been worried sick."

"Nah. *She* worried when I was in town. I wasn't smart enough to back off from bullies. She had peace of mind when I was off on my own."

He watched her listen, captivated, yet he saw her eyelids growing heavy. Cain sighed and forced himself to withdraw from her enticing warmth.

"Don't go," she began.

He kissed her silent. "Close your eyes. You need the rest in more ways than one. I'll catch a quick shower and be right back—if you don't mind me staying the night?"

"I'd like nothing better."

Kissing her again, he slipped from the bed and

walked through the cooling house to the bathroom. This time he didn't mind finding a second release alone in the shower, because he wasn't really alone. Merritt was very much with him in his imagination.

Chapter Seven

When Merritt arrived at the café the next morning, she was prepared for the inevitability of attracting way more attention than she was comfortable with on a good day. Although the lump on her forehead didn't seem as bad as last night, she still looked like she was about to hatch a baby eggplant; and, right on cue, the black eye that Cain predicted had materialized. The entire area was nasty and discolored. She'd almost wept at her reflection in the mirror. Last night she'd told Cain that if it didn't hurt so much, she would be tempted to use a roller to lather on makeup.

Cain had kissed the top of her head and assured her, "Everyone will be upset *with* you. No one is going to make fun."

"Oh, Nikki will give it a shot," she'd said, dreading that reunion most of all. The more she thought about it, the more she was convinced that Nikki had encouraged the guys to do what they'd done.

"I plan to be there," Cain had reminded her. "If she's smart, she won't start anything, because I promise, I'll finish it."

That was part of the reason why Cain wasn't with her. However, dealing with Alvie and Leroy wasn't much easier. The second they saw her, it was a toss-up as to who reacted with more drama.

"What on earth happened?" Alvie cried as Merritt passed them to hang up her jacket and change from her boots to her sneakers. She glanced into the dining room expectantly. "Where's Cain?"

"Do I need to go across the street and get them to call for the chief?" Leroy began untying the apron that he'd just fastened around his waist.

Not happy with the conclusions she thought they were jumping to, Merritt motioned for both of them to give her a chance to talk. "I was run off the road last night. You know those two overgrown juvenile delinquents that Nikki was messing with when she wasn't busy with customers?" she asked Alvie.

"Andy Hill and Kyle Zane," Alvie told Leroy, who'd been up in their apartment at the time. "Paxton people. *They* did that to you?" she asked Merritt, her expression incredulous.

"Turned right into me on my way home. It wasn't an accident, weather related or otherwise. Thank goodness, Cain noticed the time," she said for Leroy's benefit. "He came out to check on me and saw it happen."

"Did he give those punks a good scare?" Leroy asked, holding up his clenched fist.

"No, by the time he reached the road, they were all but out of sight. I can't deny that I'm relieved. Cain didn't need to get into trouble over what amounts to a pair of dimwits, especially since they work for Mr. Paxton."

"Why did they pick on you at all?" Alvie wondered aloud. "Don't take this the wrong way, honey, but they've never paid you any mind before."

True enough, Merritt thought. "Cain thought it was less about me than the truck. He felt that they assumed he was driving."

Alvie looked unconvinced. "Well, it's no secret that he's been staying at the barn while he does work for me, but there's no mistaking your size and shape for his, even at night with snow falling. No, those boys were definitely on *your* case last night. So was Nikki. I say we call the sheriff on all three of them."

"You sure there was only two in the truck, Merritt?" Leroy asked. "Wouldn't surprise me if she was riding between those two knuckleheads and ducked so she wouldn't be spotted."

Alvie latched on to that idea. "Come to think of it, she didn't announce Josh had arrived to pick her up like she usually does, sounding like Cinderella's coach has arrived. You were the only other one of us up front, Merritt, did you see his truck?"

"No," she admitted. "But I honestly didn't pay attention. And let's wait on Sheriff Gillespie. Cain took me across the street right away and we gave a report to Officer Booker. He's supposed to notify the chief and sheriff first thing this morning."

"Well, once they see you, they'll get into gear or

there'll be no more free coffee for any of that bunch," Alvie said. She finally hugged Merritt and clucked like a fretting hen. "Look at that bruise and your poor eye. You should have put an ice pack on it."

"I did for a while." Merritt figured a snow pack was almost the same thing. "It could be worse, I could have ended up with the stitches Cain should have had."

"Bite your tongue, child. Are you sure you're feeling well enough to work? You aren't having trouble seeing? What about a headache?"

"I'm fine." The truth was that she felt guilty for feeling as well as she did. She and Cain had made love again during the night, and she'd slept in his arms. Never mind Nikki, *she* was having her own personal fairy tale. "I won't even mind the extra work if Nikki runs true to form and doesn't come in."

"If she's smart, she'll never show her face in here again. I'm fed up with her," Alvie said. "I have the numbers for a couple of people that have stopped by now and again asking if we have an opening. As soon as we get this issue resolved, I'll call them."

"I'm sorry that I didn't get any baking done," Merritt told her. "But it seems that we're starting off quiet, so I'll get some biscuits made right away."

Alvie vetoed that. "No way. We'll push pancakes and waffles today. You take it easy. Leroy, you watch that she doesn't overdo bending and picking up stuff."

"I will, babe."

But things didn't stay slow at the café. With the snowfall only producing about four inches, people were out and about soon enough, and diner traffic grew non-stop. However, with Nikki definitely a no-show, Leroy rose above and beyond the call of duty and was almost as attentive and efficient as Merritt was.

Just after seven-thirty, Cain arrived. As she waited on the last drips as the coffee machine completed producing a new pot, Merritt spotted him outside stomping snow off of his boots. Every nerve ending in her body did some form of gymnastics in euphoria. She wished she could have seen his expression when he'd wakened and realized that, not only was it daylight, but his truck was gone.

The far end of the lunch counter had a few vacant seats by then and he claimed the last one by the wall. Merritt signaled Leroy that she would serve him. Leroy gave her the thumbs-up and went to bus two tables.

"Somebody should have wakened somebody," Cain murmured, narrow-eyed as she arrived with a mug and the fresh pot of coffee.

"Somebody didn't have the heart," she whispered back. Aware that her condition kept attention on her, Merritt was careful to keep her expression as neutral as her voice was low.

Cain had less luck containing himself and rubbed at his face with both hands. "You're breaking mine. Tell me it doesn't hurt as bad as it looks like it should."

"It doesn't. I'm actually thinking of having this permanently tattooed on," Merritt quipped, putting down his mug and filling it. "Everyone is being so nice."

Over his clasped hands, Cain shot her a warning look. "What did Chief Robbins have to say?"

"He rarely arrives at the station before eight."

His jaw working, Cain surveyed the room. "I take

it the rest of the help is taking her sweet time arriving, too?"

"We think that's a blessing." Merritt tapped her pencil to the order pad. "Order something. I have platters waiting on me in the kitchen."

"I'll inhale anything you put in front of me. For some reason I'm starving."

Merritt lost her struggle with trying to keep a straight face. "Behave. I'll be back shortly."

Alvie was looking worried when she arrived, but it soon changed to wry indulgence. "There I am wondering if you had a fainting spell and instead you look like the cat who won a lifetime supply of BBQ canary. Somebody tip you a Ulysses Grant?"

"Not quite. That order is for Cain," she said, slipping the ticket on the carousel. "I'm just enjoying his wounded ego. He didn't hear me take his truck this morning."

"Don't rub too much salt in that wound. Like the rest of us, he cares that you could easily be in a hospital right now—or worse." Alvie slid three plates at her. "There's your table nine. Tell Donny that strip bacon is because I'm out of Canadian bacon. The supplier says they should have more by the next delivery."

Nodding, Merritt went to deliver the plates. When she turned to fetch the coffeepot to top off mugs, she almost walked straight into Sanford Paxton.

"Oh! Excuse me, sir." She began to step around him, but he stretched out his arm to stop her.

"Good Lord, Ms. Miller."

To Merritt's dismay, he immediately slanted a malevolent look at Cain. That told her that he had known where Cain sat as soon as he'd entered, and that his first thought was to blame Cain for her injury.

"Yes," she managed, although she was shaking inside with indignation. She self-consciously brushed away a nonexistent wisp of hair from her forehead. "It's a shock to everyone." Squaring her shoulders, she tried to ignore that her heart was threatening to choke her and added, "It's only right to inform you that I reported an incident to Officer Booker last night at the police station. You see, I was run off the road by two people who'd been dining here earlier. They work for you."

Sanford Paxton's lower lip slipped forward. Not a good sign as far as Merritt was concerned.

"That's a serious accusation."

"I'm aware of that. I wish I didn't have to make it."

"I saw it happen." Cain came behind her and put his hands on her shoulders. "I'd come out from the barn because the house was dark, meaning Merritt was late returning from work."

"You let her walk at that hour?" Sanford asked. His pale blue gaze met and challenged Cain's.

"I wasn't walking, Cain kindly lent me his truck," Merritt said before he could respond. She could feel his anger emanating from him, and his fingers were biting into her shoulder bones. "It's Andy Hill and Kyle Zane, sir. We went across the street because it was snowing. I didn't want to go at all, but Cain insisted."

For the first time Sanford nodded as though he approved. "And what did they say?"

Painfully aware that every eye and ear in the place was locked on them, Merritt told him the incriminating truth. "No one has been in touch since."

To her surprise, Sanford Paxton was no more pleased with that bit of news than Cain had been. Murmurs rose around the room as diners reacted and speculated.

"That is inexcusable and you have my sincere apologies, Ms. Miller," Sanford said with a formal nod. "I'm personally going to go look into this situation. In the meantime, be assured that I will handle any and all of your medical expenses."

"I don't have any," she told him.

He looked taken aback. "A head injury is nothing to underestimate."

"I'm fine."

He sighed. "In that case, if there's any damage to the truck—"

"It's not about the truck," Cain interjected. "The point is that they did what they did to an innocent woman with reckless intent. Thank God she was cautious due to the weather and refused to do the speed limit. Otherwise, she'd have been propelled into that tree and probably died there."

The old man's coloring grew gray and then red, and his gaze flicked from Cain to Merritt and back again. "Thank God, indeed," he murmured. "Pardon me."

It was somewhat startling to see him walk out of the place, and Merritt turned to look questioningly at Cain. He responded with a "who knows?" look.

"He's not heading for his truck," someone at the window called over to the rest of the clientele, who were discussing what had just happened in their normal voices. "He's going directly to the police station!"

That sent the room abuzz. Merritt discreetly urged Cain to resume his seat—not that she thought they were fooling anyone about how things stood between them at this point—and went in back to update Alvie in case she'd missed something.

"I nearly had a coronary when I saw Cain come to stand with you," the older woman said.

You're not the only one, Merritt thought. "Did you hear? Mr. Paxton is at the police station."

"I'm proud that he went. No doubt he's just worried about a civil lawsuit. But whatever the motivation, if this resolves the situation, I'm grateful to him for doing the right thing. Now, here's Cain's breakfast," Alvie said, setting the platter on the counter.

Merritt brought the four-egg, Western-style omelet to him. "You should have let me handle that on my own," she told him as hindsight started nagging at her.

"What would that say of me if I did?"

He was right, and it was important that his grandfather saw what an upstanding man he was. "Take the truck on your way back. Your boots are probably already wet and you shouldn't work like that all day."

Cain's answering look was a caress. "All right. But I'll come to get you by eleven."

Never a clock-watcher, Cain became one that morning—and with justifiable reason. When he collected Merritt as promised, he found her all but teetering on her feet she was so tired. Then he learned that there had been no further news from the police or sheriff departments. To say he was disappointed and offended for her was an understatement.

"I don't care, really," she told him, once she noticed his silence was due to him clenching his teeth.

"Well, I do," Cain ground out. "And Sanford should be ashamed of himself. It wouldn't surprise me at all if he assured Matt Robbins and Sheriff Gillespie that he would handle the situation, and then told his two hands to just keep a low profile for a few days."

"Don't say that," Merritt entreated. "He sounded quite disturbed and sincere."

"Yeah, it was a winning performance."

"I think he's tried to show a different side of himself lately."

"Sanford Paxton has only one side and it's as black as his soul." When Merritt made no comment to that, Cain thought that she'd begun dropping off to sleep. The warm sunshine coming through the windshield certainly encouraged that. Instead he realized she was fingering the elastic on the end of her braid, no doubt the Merritt rendition of a worry stone. Sighing, he relented. "Okay, in what way do you think he's changed?"

"He's tried to be friendlier to me. He even offered to give me a lift home."

"What?" Cain tried to remember when that would have been possible.

"He was very nice," she said. "Nicer than I was. I was too upset for your history with him, although I called myself foolish for defending you," she added. "You were gone at the time. At least I thought you were."

Now remembering, Cain thought of how the old buzzard hadn't wasted much time. He couldn't blame him—Merritt was like finding an unexpected pearl in a beach of chipped and dirty shells. Spending any amount of time with her was a healing thing.

"Did you accept his offer?" he made himself ask, although he was afraid of the answer.

"No. I was still dealing with the shock of all the pain he caused you growing up," she said. She took a deep breath and expelled it. "I don't want to argue. Can't we change the subject? Nikki never showed up and it was so nice. No one had to watch what they said, we laughed, the customers were understanding when we fell a little behind…and now I'm with you, which is best of all."

Cain reached over and clasped her hand, giving it a gentle squeeze. "I do have something to show you."

She brightened immediately. "Did you finish whatever it was you said Alvie wanted you to make for the barn?"

"In a way." He turned into the driveway. The sunlight on the fresh snow was blinding as he drove up to park in front of the closed barn doors to where he didn't have to ask her to close her eyes.

"I need to invest in a pair of sunglasses," Merritt said, grimacing as she opened the door. "I'm the world's worst, constantly losing them."

"This way," Cain said when she started for the bar across the double doors. He waited for her and then tucked her against his side to protect her from the wind that continued to blast them with Arctic cold.

When they rounded the southwest side of the barn, it only took Merritt a moment before she gasped, "*A hen house?* I'm going to have my own laying hens!"

Her girlish giggle put a grin on Cain's face. He'd worked like a maniac yesterday and this morning to get it done. Ed Quinn at Quinn Hardware and

Lumber—where he'd been purchasing the materials for everything—had come out to look at his work. He was so impressed, he ended up asking him to redo his barn's roof at the family residence. He needed to start right away, and would have hated keeping her waiting on this.

"Do you like it? Look, it's even closed in on top by chicken wire to keep out every kind of predator. I'll add mesh underground to discourage varmints from trying to dig their way in as soon as the spring thaw softens the ground." He wondered if she caught it—the promise that he would still be here in the spring. He'd surprised even himself.

"I'm thrilled. Speechless." She stepped inside the coop that was every bit as big as her kitchen. "I'd been telling Alvie how I could improve our profit margin and produce healthier product by controlling what the hens eat. Thank you so, so much! Oh, you two sneaks…"

As she came to him, arms spread, Cain gave in to the hunger that had been gnawing at him since entering the café this morning. Folding her close, he sought and claimed her mouth for a deep kiss; the only thing to make it possible to ignore the wind and cold, and to make sense in their unfair world.

Murmuring in appreciation, Merritt pressed her cheek against his chest. "You make me want to curl up in your lap like a spoiled cat." She stifled a yawn. "I am so tired."

And so not spoiled. "Let's get you inside." Cain knew that for her to drop her "I'm fine" mantra, she had to be close to collapse. "You lie down while I take care of things inside."

"You're too busy with your own things to wait on me. Besides, I need to work. Alvie can't get away with serving pancakes and waffles at dinner."

"I'll make a deal with you," he said, guiding her out of the pen and toward the house. "You lie down, and if you're not up by three o' clock, I'll wake you."

Merritt relented easily, and by the time Cain drove her to back to town for the dinner shift, she looked and sounded more like herself—*and* she'd managed to make the corn bread for the chili, dinner rolls and a couple of pies.

She humbled and inspired him. He wished his grandmother could have met her as he told her about the Quinn job. No surprise, she was thrilled for him.

"Word is getting around about what good work you do. Before you know it, you're going to be turning away work—or needing a helper."

"Two jobs don't add up to a steady paycheck," he reminded her. He was afraid that she might get too many stars in her eyes. It was foolish enough for him to be harboring fantasies of a future for them.

As they were entering the café, Cain noticed the idling red coupe parked in front and the driver. It was Josh Bevans, foreman of Paxton Ranch. After spotting them, Bevans turned his face away. By now, Cain recognized Nikki's car and wondered why Bevans wasn't in his ranch truck.

Just as Cain was about to warn Merritt that Nikki might be inside, the door swung open and the young woman burst out and past Merritt. "Hey!" he snapped. Luckily, he was able to steady Merritt, even though one hand was occupied with carrying tonight's baked offerings.

"Nikki, what is your problem?" Merritt demanded.

Except for a scathing look for both of them, Nikki didn't slow her pace. She slipped and skidded over the mound of snow at the end of the sidewalk where Leroy had piled it and grabbed the truck's passenger door handle to steady herself. For once she was dressed in jeans and sneakers, which also saved her. She would never have managed that maneuver in one of her tight leather minis and stiletto heels, Cain concluded, although he half wished she had ended up on her backside.

As Bevans backed out of the slot, Nikki shot Merritt a one-finger salute.

"Very mature," Merritt noted to Cain.

"Doesn't look like you're going to have much help with the dinner service, either," Cain replied.

Upon entering the building, they met Leroy standing with his hands on his hips monitoring the whole situation. "She came for her pay," he explained. "She's leaving town. I was making sure she didn't damage something or help herself to anything she shouldn't. A lady she isn't."

"It's interesting that Josh Bevans was with her in her car," Merritt said. "You think they're both leaving?"

Leroy nodded toward the door. "Maybe he knows something."

By the time the middle-aged man in winter police

blues and a matching down-filled jacket crossed the street and entered the café, Alvie had joined the group.

"This doesn't exactly stack up to be a fair fight," Chief Matt Robbins observed and he tipped his ball cap to Alvie and shook hands with Leroy and Cain. Then he winced at Merritt and took her hand in both of his. "Miss Miller. I am sorry about what happened. How are you doing?"

"Better than I look, Chief."

Cain could feel Merritt retreat from the law enforcement officer until she was completely backed up against him. He knew she was afraid that he would start asking questions about her past and squeezed her arm in reassurance.

"Glad to hear it. Added apologies for not getting here sooner," he said, looking meaningfully at Cain. "It's been one of those days when you need to be in three places at once and even then someone gets short shrifted. But I'm just off the phone with Sheriff Gillespie, who also sends his regrets. I don't know if anyone's heard about it yet, but he had a small plane go down on the other side of the county and asked if I'd be his liaison between you and Mr. Paxton until he can get here, probably tomorrow."

"We may not need him," Alvie said. "Things seem to be working out pretty well. That was Nikki Franks who just left. She was here getting her pay before leaving town. She put those two boys up to what they did to our Merritt."

Calm, yet serious, Matt Robbins nodded. "Mr. Paxton tells me that the two gentlemen you mentioned have been fired and ordered off of the ranch. Mr.

Bevans was let go because Mr. Paxton concluded that he'd known about what happened then he'd lied about his girlfriend's involvement."

"That's faster than a jury trial," Merritt murmured.

His pleasant face relaxing into a smile, Matt Robbins asked her, "All Sheriff Gillespie will need to know now is if you'll want to press charges, Ms. Miller."

"No." She shook her head adamantly. "Mr. Paxton went beyond anything I could have asked for. All I wanted was an apology and an assurance that it wouldn't happen again—and to repair Cain's truck if there proved to be damage."

Matt lifted his eyebrows questioningly at Cain. "How is it?"

"Drivable. It had gone through eight of its nine lives when I got it."

"Sometimes I wish for the days of a good saddle horse myself. I was just told the transmission on my patrol car is shot. It isn't three years old." He shook hands again. "I'll leave you good people to your work."

As soon as the door closed behind him, Leroy mused, "How about that?"

"I would never have expected Sanford to turn out to be such a stand-up guy," Alvie said.

"Frankly, I'm happier about that than I am to be free of Nikki's troublemaking," Merritt said.

Cain could have commented on that, but held his peace. There would be time to warn her about the old man later.

"Guess I'll put on a clean apron," Leroy said, sounding resigned.

"Sorry, Leroy." Merritt patted his back. "If I thought

I could handle the dinner crowd on my own, I'd happily do it."

He pretended to chuck her under her chin. "Aw, I'm just kidding. That girl was a thorn in Alvie's side almost as much as she was yours."

Cain made an impromptu decision. "I'll be happy to stay and fill in wherever you need me," he told to Alvie. "Bus tables, wash dishes. I'd planned to stay close until you locked up anyway. Nikki and Josh may be gone, but we don't know where the other two are."

Merritt gave him a smile that made him want to corner her in the storage room for ten delicious minutes.

Leroy rubbed his hands with enthusiasm. "Now we've got a team."

"Thank you, Cain," Alvie said, pressing her hand to her chest. "You make me ashamed for ever having any doubt in you."

The bulk of the work remained on Merritt's and Leroy's shoulders, but Cain soon caught on to where he had trays of iced water and tea ready and breadbaskets warming under the heating light. While he otherwise preferred to do dishes, he bused tables when necessary and reset them. Once or twice he got a curious or wary look, but that was the extent of public awareness. Much of the evening crowd was different from the breakfast group, and it didn't appear that he knew all that many of them.

But he would know Sanford anywhere and, at dusk, when the local icon came through the door looking like the millionaire rancher that he was in a wolf-gray suede hat, jacket and boots ensemble, Cain sensed that even with this crowd, some conversations died out completely. One individual—Cain recognized him as a banker—tried to get his attention, but Sanford ignored him, his gaze settling on Merritt. Since he stayed where he was by the door, she circumspectly went to him.

Oh, Mer, don't fall prey to the Miller Moth vulnerabilities tonight.

Sanford touched the brim of his hat, the hint of a smile softening the hard angles of his weathered face. "Miss Miller."

"Good evening, Mr. Paxton. How can I help you?"

"I'm hoping that it's the other way around this time. I came by to assure you that the matter we spoke of yesterday has been resolved. The individuals who troubled you have left my property…and town."

"I saw Josh Bevans, sir. That was unexpected. I never mentioned him."

"No, you didn't. But it couldn't be helped. Nikki tried to lie to help out those two other weasels at your expense, and Josh foolishly defended her. While he's an otherwise decent foreman, I concluded that his judgment in human nature left much to be desired, so I had to cut him loose as well."

Merritt bowed her head. "I'm sorry that I cost you experienced help."

"The apologies are mine to make. I'm only grateful things didn't get worse for you." Sanford held out a set of keys to her. "As you know, the great deal of walking that you do worries me. I'd be honored if you'd accept this as a token of my sincere apology and use it for as long as you have a need. It's the truck my former employees used. I'm sure you'll recognize it parked around the side of this building. The insurance is covered on the ranch's account."

As he tried to give her the keys, Merritt clasped her hands behind her back. "That's—that's too much, sir."

Cain watched her dilemma. Unsure of what else to say or do, she looked over her shoulder and straight at him with a beseeching look. It was impossible to define, and yet in that moment, Cain felt invincible and he met the unreadable gaze of his grandfather.

What the hell are you pulling, old man?

To Merritt, he could only shrug. He had no right to influence her, particularly in regard to this.

"Miss Miller," Sanford Paxton said to regain her attention. He shook his head at some inner struggle. "Merritt…may I call you Merritt? Your decency and absence of greed is refreshing. But you have to let me do this small thing. I've let too many years and too many opportunities slip by me—or worse yet kicked them aside out of pride, stupidity and bitterness. Please let me believe—at least for a moment—that even the biggest fool can do the right thing on a rare occasion. Please."

Merritt slowly extended her hand—paused to quickly rub her it against her apron—then accepted the keys. Cain would have bet anything that at that moment, her hand was shaking like a paint-mixing machine.

"Mr. Paxton, you don't know how much I hope you mean that. I'll take very good care of your property and will return it to you just as soon as I can afford my own vehicle."

"Good evening, Merritt."

"God bless, sir."

As soon as the door closed behind him, Merritt turned, saw too many eyes on her and ducked her head shyly, shoving the keys into her apron pocket. As she wove her way between the tables, a few diners remarked on what they'd just witnessed.

"Congratulations, Merritt."

"Good for you, honey!"

"Why doesn't anything like that ever happen to me?"

"Because you *are* greedy and indecent." The questioner's dining partner elbowed him in good fun.

A few people laughed and everyone went back to their dinners. Cain turned away from the scene and waited as Merritt came to him behind the lunch counter where he'd was refilling the ice water pitcher.

"I didn't know what to do," she whispered. Like him, her back was to the dining room. "Should I have turned it down?"

"That's not for me to say."

"Which means I should have. But it seemed as though he was trying so hard to make a point."

"He's taken with you."

She made a soft sound of disgust. "Look at me. And he's your *grandfather.*"

"And hates every second of that awareness...and the knowledge that he's old." Cain knew he was disappointing her and tried to see things from her perspective. "My truck is unreliable. Plus with this new job, getting you home at midday and driving you back would be a problem."

"I don't mind the walking."

Standing shoulder to shoulder, he used that privacy to stroke the backs of his fingers over her hand as she reached for the pitcher. "I do."

That was the last word on the subject until they headed home. They were late getting away from the café what with Alvie and Leroy wanting their own recap of Sanford's surprise visit, and then they all went outside to see the white, plain, late-model vehicle.

Now Cain was following her into the driveway. Seeing her silhouetted by his headlights, she looked like a child behind the wheel, and it struck him that he'd been wrong to think Andy and Kyle had been wanting to get at him the other night. It had been her all along.

She parked where he had last night, near the back stairs. He could have parked beside her, but was reluctant to assume anything. He parked at the double barn doors, as he had been up until last night.

When she got out of the truck, she inadvertently triggered the lights and automatic lock with the remote a few times before laughing at herself. He stayed beside his truck and smiled that anyone in this day and age wasn't yet comfortable with that type of key.

She shrugged away her embarrassment. "Sensitive things."

"You'll get used to it."

She tilted her head, a question in her eyes that he could see even in the moonlight.

"I'm going to have a glass of wine. You could join me."

"I'll want to stay."

"That was my plan."

Inside she turned on the lights and shivered. Cain felt the chill, too, although it affected him less. With both of them away all day, neither of them had been around to feed the stove and the house had cooled off.

"I'll tend to it," he said.

They moved in opposite directions like a married couple who knew their individual routines and chores to make the whole work. He liked how that felt, the stability of It. It felt like home.

When they reconnected in the bedroom—where she left the lights off as before, relying only on the illumination from the kitchen—she put the wine goblets on their night tables and knelt on the bed to turn back the comforter and puff up the four pillows. They'd already peeled off their coats and boots and left everything at the back door.

She scooted around to lean against her pillows and took a sip of her wine. "Ah, I so need this. What an incredible, but long day." She flexed her socked feet before drawing up her knees and half turning to him. When he picked up his own glass and settled beside her, she touched her goblet to his. "Thank you for all you did—I mean on top of the huge job with the coop. Helping with the café…I know it isn't your thing."

It wasn't Leroy's thing, either, he thought, sipping the cabernet. It was her and Alvie's. But he didn't mind it. "I was glad to help, especially when I can see how happy it makes you."

"That's why I was afraid I'd ruin things by accepting your grandfather's gift."

Cain dealt with an instinctive spasm of resentment. "Can we leave him outside that door?" He slipped his hand to her nape and gently coaxed her head toward his. "Three's a crowd," he said against her lips.

The wine was heady after a demanding day. But her kiss was equally potent, fanning a spark deep in his belly. "That's the only thing they should serve with wine."

Although she murmured softly in agreement, Merritt put down her glass and unwound the elastic band from her hair. Cain knew she continued to wrestle with her decision, tiptoeing through their minefield-riddled relationship, too.

As she unbraided her hair, he unsnapped the top button on her green Christmas sweater. He leaned forward and kissed the shallow valley between her breasts. "I didn't mean to hurt your feelings."

"No. I understand."

Did she? "Mer...I may seem like the most confident man on the planet, determined to do things my way, but nothing could be further from the truth. Try to understand...I just found you. I'm still hanging on to the high of learning that you really want me, see someone of value despite what others think. But I can already see seeds being sown that could change your mind."

Merritt stroked his cheek. "Your grandfather isn't trying to come between us."

Now that her hair was free, he filled his hands with it and breathed in the clean, subtle fragrance of her shampoo. "I want you to be *mine*. Even as I struggle with believing I'm what you need."

His next kiss was all possessiveness, born of despair as much as desire. Merritt gave herself completely to it and him, until the first pang of his urgency eased. Then she took his glass and set it beside hers.

Turning back to him, she wrapped her arms around his neck, which brought their bodies flush. To get closer, she slid her leg between his and gazed deeply into his eyes.

"This is too important to let you make all of the decisions." In between her coaxing words, she brushed her lips against his—soothing yet enticing at the same time. "And for the record, I knew I was yours from the moment you touched me."

Filled with emotions that threatened to overwhelm him, Cain rolled onto his back and drew her completely over him. He'd carried saddles that weighed more than her, and yet just as their aligned bodies suited each other in a unique fit, he knew she'd spoken some undeniable truth.

His hands worshipped her as he gripped her hips to rub her against the need building in his groin. Their deep kiss matched the slow, undulating dance of their bodies. The whisper of their clothing against the bedding served as their words.

I can't stop.

Don't stop.

Here.

That way.

When he slid his hands along the sides of her breasts, then over them, he could feel her nipples through her shirt and bra. He drank in her encouraging murmurings. It took only seconds for him to open the rest of her sweater and tug down her bra to give her what she was wordlessly asking for.

She arched into his mouth and moaned as he suckled then lathed her with his tongue. Cocooned by her hair, they created their own fragile sanctuary of two.

"Kiss me," he groaned, seeking her mouth.

She did, at the same time feverishly working on the snaps of his flannel shirt. The instant their naked flesh touched, they went absolutely still, savoring the reunion.

As their shaky breaths merged, Cain rasped, "I've been wanting this all day. Last night was too short."

There wasn't time or patience to remove all of their clothes. It was enough to lower this and push that out of the way. Their hands worked with canny cooperation that seemed to only charge the highly erotic atmosphere.

Then Cain probed, tentatively at first, and afterward deeper, until she'd taken all of him, their shallow breaths transforming into thin, short pants. Merritt clung to him as though to a life itself and used her cheek to stroke his jawline, her nose to nuzzle his collarbone.

In a moment of acute consciousness, their gazes met. He saw that their thoughts had merged on the same wavelength. They'd become aware of the risk they'd invited by taking things this far without protection. If anyone had a full grasp of the difficult repercussions that could emerge from this, they did. Yet neither of them did anything, except to tighten their embrace.

"That's...so good," she whispered.

"You are," he replied. Taking her mouth with his, he raced her to climax.

Chapter Eight

"The one thing we're aiming for here is to always have each others' backs," Merritt said to the new waitress, Sally Evers.

That was a policy that she, Alvie and Leroy agreed was vital as they worked on replacing Nikki. Business was continuing to grow. They'd hired Mimi Vinton the week after Thanksgiving. There would be no more tolerating Nikki's "everybody for himself" approach to her job. And here it was only the day before Christmas Eve and indications were that things would go as well with Sally as they were with Mimi. A thirty-year-old divorcée, Sally indicated that she would learn fast and carry her weight. So far, she'd earned their appreciation by showing up time. It appeared that Sally had moved back in with her widowed but energetic mother, who could take over with Sally's two young sons and see they got off to school on time when they weren't allowed to sleep later due to Christmas break.

As she continued her instructing between customers, Merritt pointed out to Sally how Mimi was also starting a new pot of coffee. "We don't leave each other high and dry if we find we're pouring the last cup of something. It takes a few seconds, but you'll get repaid for that in a harmonious working atmosphere, believe me. Oh, and if the customer getting that last cup doesn't like that stronger cup of coffee, replace it free of charge."

Blonde, with her shoulder-length hair in a ponytail, Sally looked and acted younger than twenty-five-year-old Mimi. "I had a chance to follow Mimi while you were on the phone. She's awesome. Twenty-five, no boyfriend, going to school full-time—she has her act together."

Merritt nodded, but didn't add any information that she'd gleaned from Mimi's job application and since working with her. What Mimi wanted Sally to know, she could tell her in her own time. "We're all no-pressure people here. The work is demanding enough without adding to that. Besides, if you're having a good time, the shift flies by." Merritt pointed to the elderly couple on her side of the room who'd just taken their usual table by the window. "That's Mr. and Mrs. Ford. Their pace is slow, but they're sharp in every other way. Mrs. Ford will ask for hot tea and Mr. Ford will want hot water with lemon. Don't mistake that for a senior moment. That's an old-timers' regularity recipe."

"Oh. *Oh.* Okay."

As Sally went off to care for the Fords, Merritt went back to the kitchen, where Alvie was fanning herself with the spatula as she stood over the griddle monitoring an order of bacon, ham and hash browns. Business was on an upswing even from Thanksgiving and Alvie was showing the effects.

"Do you need me to relieve you so you can sit down for a few minutes?" Merritt asked.

"No, but I'll take a diet whatever from the fountain."

Merritt immediately got the lime-flavored beverage for her, knowing she didn't like any of the colas. "Success has its price," she observed through the opening to the dining room.

"We're going to have to do more than paint over the weekend while we're shut down." Alvie worriedly shook her head. "We're going to have to talk about looking for a short-order cook and at least one more person for the lunch counter."

"Leroy *is* looking a little overwhelmed himself. Thank goodness these new girls are as good as Dara and Lorie are during the lunch shift. Where are these customers coming from?"

"I heard Whitfield's Dairy Barn shut down," Alvie said, referring to the fast-food stop in the next small town eastward. "Then our competition on the interstate has changed hands again and I hear the food is inedible. Don't discount your blessed baking. We could add a bakery showcase and sell out daily if we wanted to kill ourselves."

Yes, they did have increasing opportunities here, but would need more help. And Merritt had been eyeing the vacant store next door every time she parked and passed it on her way here. She was hoping to have a chance to talk to Alvie on Christmas when they got together again about expanding the café.

"I have to get back up front, but I wanted to let you know that today at lunch, I'll relieve Leroy here on the griddle or the counter, whichever he prefers, while you take your break. I'm only going home for a little while once this crowd eases up. I'll feed the stove and get the last of my orders out of the fridge—and hopefully not forget my backup dough from the freezer. Then I'll be right back."

"You're sure you're up to it?" Alvie asked, although she looked hopeful. "I know you're lots younger, but you sure are giving your poor body a workout lately. Whatever vitamin pill you're taking, I want two."

"Not to worry." Merritt stroked her perspiration-damp back. "I'm most definitely fine."

As she drove to the house in the Paxton Ranch pickup two hours later, Merritt was humming the Christmas carol she'd heard from the stereo speaker outside of Hughes Pharmacy. She couldn't believe she was in such a good mood and had so much energy despite the crazy pace they were all keeping these days. Granted, her hip was protesting more with every cold front that barreled down from Canada or the Arctic, but her euphoric heart was compensating for that.

Life with Cain was unfolding like a dream come true. They were virtually living together now, although they were both working so many hours, they were often only sleeping in the same bed. But it was heavenly to drop off to sleep in the arms of someone who claimed his day and night revolved around her.

As she pulled into the driveway, Merritt was delighted to see a familiar black truck there. She had no idea where Cain was working these days. He'd mentioned a job in Whitman and somewhere south of the interstate that meant nothing to her, due to the fact that while she'd lived here for a couple years, she had yet to find the time or means to explore the area. She was just grateful that there had been no more talk of worrying over where his next paycheck would come from, or not being good enough for her. Of course, there hadn't been any "I love you" spoken, either, but he'd shown her—they'd shown each other countless times every day. She thought of that classic song from the Broadway musical *Carousel,* "If I Loved You." Her romance with Cain seemed star-crossed like Julie and Billy's, but they were determined to do a better job at communicating than those fictional characters.

Parking beside Cain's old truck, she couldn't help but keep a smile on her face as she climbed the stairs and opened the back door. "Hi! It's— Hello," she said with a chuckle as she came face-to-face with Cain, who seemed to be on his way out already. What a nice surprise. Are you…leaving?"

"Yeah. You're home early."

"Nice to see you, too." Merritt rose on tiptoe and kissed his cheek. "We're busy and I promised to work through lunch, but I needed the rest of my orders and to pick up more dough from the freezer." She tilted her head and inspected him more closely. His coloring seemed normal, yet he seemed to be not himself somehow. That was it—he was standing oddly. "Is everything all right?"

His grimace was all chagrin. "I had an accident."

"Are you hurt? The truck didn't look—"

"I wasn't in the truck. I was on a horse."

From their various conversations, Merritt knew that he hadn't been on a horse in years. "What were you—? Sit down. You really don't look yourself."

"Sitting is the biggest problem." He placed his hands on the small of his back only to flex and wince. "I got bucked off my mount into a pile of firewood. I'd just come home to change into jeans with...less ventilation."

Merritt formed a silent O with her lips. "That must have been some fall. Do you need to go to the doctor for a tetanus shot or something?"

"Nah. Except for sporting a map of Asia on my ass, and having my brains rattled, I'm okay. I'll just be stiff for a few days."

Relieved that things weren't worse, Merritt put down the tote on the nearest chair and gave him a hug. "I don't know if I should trust that whitewashed version of things, but I'm grateful there wasn't any blood or broken bones involved. But whose horse were you on? Do the people where you're doing a job have horses?"

He looked torn. "Yes, a number of them. And staying *on* a horse *is* my job. I'm trying out at the ranch."

Of all the things she could have guessed, that one wouldn't have been on the list. Merritt lifted her eyebrows. She didn't pretend not to know which one he was referring to. "You...at Paxton Ranch. That's some news. What does 'trying out' mean?" More importantly, why was he keeping it a secret from her?

"Present appearances aside, while I can handle a horse, I don't have much experience with cattle."

Merritt considered that for a moment. "If you're taking Andy or Kyle's spot, they didn't strike me as being all that accomplished with them or anything else, either."

"Officially, yeah, I'm replacing one of them. Unofficially, I'm supposed to be replacing Josh Bevans. Only I didn't feel right about Sanford bringing in a total greenhorn—especially a grandson—and immediately giving me Josh's authority. It will look better and probably work better with the other hands if I earn the position."

Merritt couldn't be more surprised, but also elated. "That's…that's great. When did this happen?"

"The day after I finished the job for Ed Quinn. I had a few other small things lined up, but there wasn't much money in those. I started to worry. I even thought about reenlisting."

"Cain!"

The idea scared her to death and she had to turn away. While she understood that someone had to fill that need, and she had confidence in his abilities—he'd survived two enlistments with several deployments, for pity's sake—he was a decade older than new recruits and he'd already given so much of himself. Most importantly, she thought with admitted selfishness, he would undoubtedly be gone for such long stretches of time. Months. Maybe years.

She felt his hands on her upper arms and he turned her around. Then he touched a kiss to her forehead.

"I said I thought about it. It's not like I did it."

"No," she said, her tone edged with irony. "Your second self-abusive idea was to go to the man who hurt you more than anyone else in your life."

"Actually, he came to me. Somewhat. I was outside the recruiter's station in Helena—"

"You were all the way up there?"

"It's only a couple of hours' drive."

More like Russian Roulette with his truck. Merritt bit her tongue to keep from saying more, but his admission told her how disturbed he was about his employment situation.

"Sanford was there on business," Cain continued, although he looked like he expected her to interrupt at any second. "He stopped me as I was crossing the street to go in."

"He must have been as upset as I am."

Cain's expression was skeptical, but he didn't come out and deny it. On the other hand, he didn't continue with the story, either. *Now what?* Merritt wondered.

"I'm already shaken to the core," she told him. "Add that you thought it was good to keep such a big secret and I— Please, stop keeping me in the dark."

He put his arms around her and stroked her back, and when he spoke, he sounded like he was telling a child a bedtime story. "He asked me what I thought I was doing, and I told him that I was trying to make a life for myself and the girl I wanted to marry. I explained how you worked hard enough for two people trying to improve the hand life had dealt you, and that

I was trying to do the same, but that things didn't seem to be working out as I'd hoped."

"And he said…?" she asked, her heart in her throat.

"He said that my honesty and fortitude had shown more character and courage than he had displayed in all of his seventy-nine years." Cain went quiet as though tasting the moment again. "He explained that he had a grandson whom he'd taught to despise him—and he didn't know how to change that."

Merritt felt her breath escape her like a tapped pressure valve. "Oh, Cain. He did! I *knew* something had changed."

Bemused, he took hold of both lapels on her jacket and gently but firmly lifted her to her tiptoes. "You pocket-size piece of misdirected magic. You're too optimistic for your own good, when you're not putting funny ideas in people's heads."

He kissed her in a way that discounted his mockery and exposed his adoration. Merritt filled her hands with the back of his jacket and adored him back.

Once they decided it was time to breathe again, Cain tucked her head under his chin and rocked her soothingly. "I did tell him that I didn't need a grandfather."

"No," she moaned, pulling away. "The man bares his soul—"

Cain touched a finger to her lips. "I *said* that I didn't care about that or want anything for myself, but that I wanted something for you. Mer, forgive me, but I told him how you got hurt. I told him about the scum who did that to you, and I promised that if he would find out if you had any need to fear the past, I would dig fence posts on his land for the rest of my life if he wanted me to."

Merritt's flicker of hope died and she slumped against the back door in defeat. What he'd done, what he'd risked, reminded her too much of his parents' story. "You shouldn't have. You gave him the only justification he needs to make him question reaching out to you. He'll never give you his support or blessing now."

Cain put his fingers under her chin and forced her to meet his gaze. "You're wrong, my love. He made a few calls and hired a private detective. The report came over the weekend. I was saving it for you as a Christmas present. Dennis didn't die, but he is in prison. He was caught soliciting a minor. During the investigation of that they found enough pedophilia crap on his computer to keep him locked up for a long time."

Merritt closed her eyes, all but weak with relief. It was over and she was free. What's more, no other innocents would suffer at his hands. "Did the investigator by chance learn where Stanley is?"

"He did. Stanley is living with another woman. The guy described a sorry state of affairs."

She nodded. Stanley wasn't going to change either, and there would always be women who thought some man was better than no man.

Free, she thought again and smiled at Cain. "I'm so grateful. I should call Mr. Paxton, shouldn't I? I have to—"

"Tell me that you love me."

Certain that her heart stopped, Merritt savored the moment. "I do," she whispered before launching herself at him. "I so love you."

* * *

She felt like she was walking on air and Merritt wished she didn't have to return to work. But too soon she and Cain yielded to their consciences and parted. One thing was for certain—she couldn't wait to get home that night. There were so many more things she wanted to ask Cain, and hear about.

In a private moment with Alvie, she couldn't resist confiding the part about Cain's hopeful agreement with Sanford. Alvie promptly dropped a dozen eggs on the concrete floor, which had Merritt deciding to wait for a better moment to fill her in on the rest. As she helped clean up the mess, she swore her to secrecy until Cain felt comfortable to go public. That would be soon, she added, since surely the ranch hands had family and friends around town. It amazed her that they'd been tight-lipped this long.

When she finally did arrive home after closing, she found Cain not in but on the bed, fast asleep. No doubt he'd thought he would nap until she arrived, but clearly the day had taken its toll on him.

After lowering herself to the edge of the mattress, she leaned closer to nibble gently on his earlobe. It took little more for him to rouse and reach for her.

"Sorry, sweetheart. Dozed off." He checked the time on the clock on the nightstand. "Jeez, I slept that long?"

"How do you feel?"

"My age," he muttered with a rueful smile. "The way this job is going, I'm not looking forward to what thirty-four feels like."

Like the marines wouldn't have been every bit harder on him, she thought to herself. She stroked his hair, her gaze on the remains of his last injury. "When will that be—this thirty-four business?" she asked, trying to keep things light.

"February." He drew her closer for a tender kiss. "What are you doing—trying to figure out if we're compatible? Too late. You're stuck with me."

She smiled. "It sounds like you've been home for a while?"

"Two hours. It would have been sooner, but Sanford asked me to come to the house. He wanted to show me around." He gingerly scooted up to a sitting position and adjusted the pillows behind him.

Merritt could just imagine Cain's hesitation over that, and yet she understood Sanford's desire to accelerate the pace of their reconnection. They'd lost more than thirty-three years already. "Did that include showing you any photos of your father?"

Cain nodded, his look thoughtful. "I saw his room. Sanford has kept it the way it was when he died."

"That's understandable...but sad. Do you look like him?"

"Some." Cain studiously took the band off of Merritt's hair and started unbraiding it. "His hair was more this color, but I have his face shape and his nose and mouth. My mother's coloring and eyes."

Merritt let her gaze drift over him, trying to separate those features. "They must have been striking people."

"But so young. Younger than us."

"Did Mr. Paxton mention your grandmother at all?"

"I saw several photos of her in the house. She died young, too, but he said hers were medical issues unconnected with my father's birth. He didn't seem to want to go into details at the moment. I do know my father was raised by the housekeeper—at least that's what my mother had told her mother."

Merritt wondered about Cain's twin brother. Did Sanford name him? Where was he buried and did Cain ever feel the need to go to the grave? These were all questions that made her ache for him, but she sensed tonight wasn't the time for them.

"Your grandfather has been alone a long time," Merritt said, thinking of so many lost years. "What's he doing for Christmas?"

"The subject didn't come up. I was too busy saying 'no' to things."

"What kind of things?" Merritt experienced a pang of worry and hoped he wasn't going to let his independent streak hurt this fragile reconnection.

"He wanted to give me Josh Bevans's truck. He wanted to start me with a foreman's salary. He wanted us to move into the house with him."

Merritt relaxed. That was all understandable to her. Excessive enthusiasm was natural. Overcompensation. But Sanford didn't yet understand the proud yet modest and moderate man he was dealing with. "Naturally, you only want to be paid for your value, but you do see that he's wanting to make up for all of the birthdays and holidays that he's missed?"

"That's his problem. And home is here."

She laid her hand against his heart, taking as much reassurance from its steady beat as his words. She would go anywhere he asked, but she could only imagine the kind of place Sanford Paxton lived. "Is it an intimidating mansion?" Just talking about it had her feeling the urge to fidget and do something to keep the shakes away.

"No, you'd probably love it—it's what they call in these parts a great lodge. All stone and logs. Fantastic kitchen. Massive fireplace that you could put ten of your stoves in."

A lodge sounded better than a mansion, but the size once again left her intimidated. "He probably has live-in help?"

"No, a service." Cain wound a length of her hair around his finger and drew her toward him. "One of the hand's wife cooks for him now and again. She fills the freezer and he can stick whatever he wants in the microwave when he doesn't have an engagement somewhere."

"I think we should invite him to Christmas dinner."

"He probably has plans."

"Is the house decorated?"

"No, but that doesn't mean anything."

It said a great deal to her. "It wouldn't hurt to ask," Merritt insisted. "Do you work tomorrow?"

"Cattle don't know it's Christmas Eve."

"Please ask," she entreated, refusing to be undermined by his teasing. "Or I'll call him from Alvie's. Have you written his number down somewhere?" She figured he did to report in if he was having truck trouble and running late, or because Sanford would want him to have it "just because."

"He gave me his business card...and one for you," he said, a note of resignation entering his voice. He gestured toward his billfold on the night table. "It's in there. Help yourself. I guess I really need to break down and get a cell phone," he continued, watching her waste no time in getting one of the cards. "You need to be able to reach me, too, since I'm farther away."

With an impish smile, Merritt got up and went to the living room, where she picked up a package among the several under the tree. She presented it to him.

Cain's expression was a unique mixture of pleasure and something she couldn't put her finger on as he lifted the decorated lid and saw the cell phone inside.

"I charged the battery already," she told him. "And it comes with a case where you can fasten it to your belt. I thought that would be safer than tucking it in a pocket where it could fall out. I was thinking of you on ladders, but that really seems an equally good idea now if you're going to be riding a horse."

"Yeah, it does." He had a whimsical smile on his face and leaned over to kiss her. "Thank you. That was more than generous. Did you get yourself one, too?"

"Not yet. I do plan to with my next paycheck. We'll have to transfer this one into your name if you agree to keep it. Then I can set myself up with one."

His smile turned to one of satisfaction as he leaned over to open the night table's drawer. Lifting out a similar box, he offered it to her. "I haven't had time to charge it yet."

Now Merritt understood and laughed appreciatively. "Is this account in your name?"

"You guessed it."

"Well, then why don't we make it easier on each other and leave things the way they are?" Both cells were black, so it wasn't like color was a concern. "Except you take the case with the belt loop."

"I don't mind if I do."

After glancing down at the embossed business card, Merritt borrowed Cain's phone. "Before I lose my courage," she told him.

Sanford Paxton's phone rang twice, then three times. On the fourth ring, she got a recorded message. She didn't recognize the speaker's voice. At the sound of the anticipated beep, she spoke.

"Mr. Paxton, hi. This is Merritt. Cain's Merritt?" she added, suddenly shy. She won a small smile from Cain with that. "I'm sorry to call this late, but I'm only just home from work myself. I wanted you to know that we're having a small get-together here on Christmas Day. Lunch, nothing formal. No doubt you're already committed elsewhere, but if you change your mind, please know you're most welcome. Or for coffee and dessert later maybe. Merry Christmas!"

When she disconnected, she put the phone on the night table beside the other one. "I feel better now."

Drawing her completely against him, Cain murmured against her lips, "Let me tell you what would make me feel better."

When Cain joined Merritt in the kitchen on Christmas morning, he was moving more like his usual self, but he still had to stretch kinks out of his body. He was dressed only in his briefs and carrying his clothes to the shower. She felt the familiar swelling of her heart that somehow also simultaneously became a lump in her throat. He was her miracle, magnificent and so caring with her. She would never get used to the idea that he could be in love with her.

"Merry Christmas," she murmured.

"Ho, ho, ho to you." He came behind her and planted a kiss on the side of her exposed neck.

She reached up to caress his cheek, still almost whisker-free, although he had yet to shave. "Did you sleep well?"

"Well enough."

"Poor darling. Is Asia giving you problems?"

"Cute. Wrong side of the anatomy." He nestled himself against her making it impossible to miss his reaction to being close to her. "I was hoping to do some stocking stuffing before you left me this morning."

Her lips twitched. "It was tempting, but then I'd be racing to get everything done in time." She poured him a mug of coffee. "Here. I thought you'd like to take that with you as you shower."

"You make it too easy for me." He stroked his hand along her side and uttered a guttural purr. "You are as soft as you look. And lovely."

She hoped so, since she'd bought her outfit and dressed with him in mind. Today, she wore her hair loose with simple combs holding the sides from her face. She had chosen a red, long-sleeved sweaterdress that's softness did rather make her feel like a member of the feline family.

"Thank you," she said, leaning back against him.

"I thought you might like to dress that up with a little sparkle." He held a black satin box in front of her.

Merritt stared at it. "What did you do? I only got you the phone, Cain."

"You shouldn't even gotten me that much. You do too much for me as it is."

"Open it, please. I have to keep stirring the gravy so it doesn't end up with lumps."

He did, exposing a pair of elegant gold earrings. "They call that style Lovers' Knot."

"How romantic. They're the most beautiful things I've ever seen." She routinely wore the original studs she'd gotten about fifteen years ago when she'd first had her ears pierced. They were the only real gold she owned. "Will you take these out and put those in for me?" she asked, tilting her head to give him access to her right ear. She didn't want to ruin the gravy she was making for his breakfast.

Cain hesitated. "Here, give me that spoon and you do it. I'm afraid of either dropping the earring or poking you with it."

She did and then wrapped her arms around his waist. "You're determined to pull me out of my shell one way or another. These are going to attract way too much attention for a wallflower like me—and lots of questions."

"It's about time everyone else sees what I do." After kissing her again, he went for his shower.

Alvie and Leroy came a little later, this time laden with wrapped gifts instead of a tree. There was also another jug of wine. They raved over the aromas wafting through the house, especially from the prime rib. The next thing they noticed were Merritt's earrings.

Leroy whistled. "Cain, old boy, you done *good*."

"They call the design Lovers' Knot," Merritt whispered to Alvie.

"What I want to know is why hard work makes you prettier every day?" Alvie feigned disgust as she ran her hands over her lavender velour warm-up suit. "For as many years as I've been plugging away over my griddle, all I have to show for it is grayer hair and wider hips."

Laughing, Merritt reached for her left hand to lead her to the kitchen. When something poked her palm, she looked down and yelped. "Alvie! Cain, look!"

Now preening, Alvie held out her freshly manicured hand to show off an opal and diamond ring. "And I'll have you know that is platinum gold."

"Well, you finally did it," Cain said to Leroy as they shook hands.

Although the older man thanked him, he said with some resignation, "Thing is, she won't marry me. But she agreed to wear my ring and show the world she belongs to me."

"Which is plenty." Alvie waved at her face as though experiencing a hot flash. "What if we take vows, and the next thing I know you're making eyes at another woman? Divorce would be too embarrassing to contemplate at my age."

Sharing an exaggerated look with Cain, Leroy held his hands skyward. "I've been crazy about the woman for nine years. If she can't trust me now, I don't stand a chance."

"This still calls for a celebration." Patting his shoulder, Cain went to pour.

Once the men were out of earshot, Alvie said to Merritt, "As much as I love those earrings, I was hoping you'd be wearing a ring, too."

Merritt watched Cain, thinking how handsome he looked in his new white Western shirt with the mother-of-pearl snaps and his best jeans. She wanted to assure Alvie of how happy she was, *they* were, but had to demur. "It does seem like we've been through a great deal together, and yet it hasn't even been two months since we met. Come check the roast with me and give me your input on what you and Leroy call rare. I love it any which way, but Cain says he's one of those 'Call me when it's charcoal' men."

After they'd had their toast, Merritt gave Alvie and Leroy their bagged gifts. Alvie pulled out an azure-blue, rhinestone-studded tunic top, which had her bouncing on the couch with excitement.

"For that trip you two better take to Hawaii," Merritt said.

"That's exactly what crossed my mind."

"That color will make your eyes pop, pumpkin," Leroy said.

He then lifted a boxed watch from his bag. "Aw, Merritt," he drawled. "You tired of looking at my duct-taped watchband?"

Feigning seriousness, she nodded. "I've also seen you peering at the numbers. That one has a bigger face and clearer digits."

"You're a sweetheart. Open yours." Leroy indicated the one on the edge of the coffee table. "We tested every brand in the store."

It was the biggest box in the room. Ripping off the paper, Merritt gasped at the picture of the portable AM/FM radio and disc player. Then she chided Leroy. "I was going to send you home for forgetting your radio. You are so smooth. I can't tell you how much this is going to be used. I really missed the music after

Thanksgiving. My cassette player is fine for its age and what I can play on it, but I noticed Cain hasn't asked me to dance once when Mozart has been on."

They all laughed and Cain did a mock mea culpa, beating his chest.

Alvie signaled to him. "There, darlin'. That's for you from us."

"Merritt's the one who should get gifts, not me."

"It's just a hug, Cain. You're coming to be like a nephew to me," Alvie said. "Now stop acting like you're the first person in history not to like presents."

As he reached for the package, Merritt told them, "We had a good laugh when we exchanged presents and found we'd bought each other cell phones. Two of the last people in the world without them, too."

"How about that? You're already thinking like a couple," Alvie replied. "You do need them. I think that was sweet."

Cain tore at the wrapping to find blue-jean shirts in his size. "You couldn't have chosen better," he said. He carried them immediately to the bedroom and returned with two packages. A small jewelry-size one was handed to Alvie. The flat one he gave to Leroy.

Alvie's box held a gold rose pin, which had her cooing. "My...won't I look fine? You've got competition now, Merritt."

Leroy had opened his CD by then and let out a hoot. "This is their new one. We're going to cut the rug, Alvie baby. Let's warm up your music box, Merritt."

While Merritt left him and Cain to set up her stereo, she urged Alvie to use the bathroom mirror to put on her pin. She, in turn, checked things in the kitchen.

When Alvie emerged, she had her hands on her hips and was sashaying. "I don't know why I've never worn more bling," she said. "I sure look good in it."

Things stayed lively thanks to Alvie, who never ran out of conversation. Her cheerful chatter also gave Merritt plenty of opportunity to watch the clock. They danced to Leroy's new CD, and then argued about what station had the best country-western music on the radio.

Merritt delayed dinner as long as possible, hoping that Sanford would drive in. Cain appeared willing to pretend that he didn't notice, but when even he was raising his eyebrows at her, she gave up and announced that dinner was served.

She was happy with the way things turned out—the fried goat cheese and raspberry vinaigrette salad was a refreshing starter. There were slices of roast to please every preference. Everyone enjoyed the small buffet table with various ingredients for the baked potatoes, and the fresh asparagus and baby carrots were spring-fresh surprises from the Rio Grande Valley.

With that bounty of food, it was inevitable that conversation turned to the café. While they agreed that the new waitresses were going to work out well, Leroy worried whether they would get everything they'd planned to improve the place done. Only Lorie and Dara from the midday crew were coming to help with the painting tomorrow. Sally needed to drive her sons to spend the rest of the holiday with their father, but could come Saturday, and Mimi had a commitment out of town that she only explained as something she'd made before she took the job.

They were closing the café until Monday so they

could repaint the entire place, including the kitchen and storeroom. They'd also discussed making a few improvements to make better use of space and doing other cosmetic enhancements to make it more appealing for evening dining.

Suddenly, Alvie put down her fork. "Merritt, honey, before we go any further with this planning, I just have to say my piece. I think the final decision on what we do with what and move to where should be yours."

Merritt looked from her to Leroy and saw something was definitely up. "Because…?"

"I want you to take over the café. Not eventually. Now. This food…your baking…you're too talented to waste your gift by waiting tables and the business is there now. It's time to cultivate that into faithful customers before someone else notices and steals them away from us."

A myriad of thoughts and emotions zipped through Merritt's mind and she had to put down her fork, too. "I know you want to travel, and I thought you'd want me to manage things when you do. I'll be happy to. But…I don't have the kind of savings to buy your business. I wish I did."

"I don't need you to buy me out." Alvie chuckled as she shook her head. "Child, I've got all I need to travel or otherwise live comfortably. And it's not like I have any family to leave things to. Leroy, he has his kids taken care of, with what he banked when he sold his place. My idea is that we get a lawyer to draft up something that gives you the business now and the building when I'm gone."

Knowing "the building" consisted of two two-story stores had Merritt reaching for her wine to stop a coughing fit. "Alvie!" she wheezed. "That's crazy."

"Not from where I'm sitting. Honey, you know the place needs more than the good painting that we're planning, though heaven knows as long as it's been, the customers will think we replaced the building with a new one. But seriously, the place needs expansion. I've been trying to find the energy to do that for ages. Every holiday I have to turn away business, as you know, because we don't have a banquet room for parties and events. The space next door isn't earning me any rent standing empty and it's just the right size if you wanted to try a salad bar, or even a luncheon buffet if you wanted. You're young enough to apprentice an assistant baker or chef to help you or split shifts with you so you wouldn't be having to put in the hours we both do now. And Leroy and I will be there to get you through the beginning, and between trips. Won't we, honey?"

"Sure." Leroy barely looked up from his plate. "Whenever you need us."

"All we'd ask is to keep living upstairs when we're in town. Gotta have someplace to park and recuperate."

"That goes without saying," Merritt replied, still in a daze. Then the full effects of their gesture struck her and she grabbed her napkin to cover her face. She was about to burst into tears.

Cain left his chair and crouched beside her. "Mer, don't cry. You'll scare them. Hell, you'll scare me."

"I'm sorry, but...first Mr. Paxton gives me the truck, then there's *you* and everything...and now this?" She choked, fearing that saying the words would make them true. "Something must be going on. Am I about to wake up from a drug-induced coma and find myself back in Jersey in a hospital?"

The others laughed with relief and Cain removed the napkin from her to kiss her soundly.

"That's real," he murmured, his gaze saying much more.

"You've become my girl," Alvie assured her, her own eyes filling. "Don't you know that?"

"I do now," Merritt replied, rising to go hug her. "But I don't know what I did to deserve you. Any of you."

Chapter Nine

When Merritt closed the front door for the last time just before nine o'clock that night, the house looked much different. Gone was the Christmas tree that Merritt had hoped would last to Twelfth Night, or at least to New Year's. But the pine had become too dry to safely keep in the house and, thanks to everyone's help, the ornaments were packed away in their new containers and the lights were removed and tied in bundles.

The kitchen was cleaned up with only a tray of holiday cookies out, since they didn't require refrigeration like some of the sweets did. Merritt returned there as Lady Antebellum's hit about a tortured love played on the stereo. There was no denying that everyone had enjoyed themselves, and they had much to be grateful for, so Merritt didn't know why she was unable to overcome the melancholia that pulled at her.

"Here, you could probably use this," Cain said, handing her a goblet with a few sips of wine in it.

"I don't really," she told him. She resisted pressing her hand to her tummy where butterflies or something were warning her against it and put down the goblet on the counter. She did need something to do with her hands, though, as she slipped them around his shoulders. "But I do owe you an apology for doubting you about your grandfather. I never dreamed he would turn us down."

"Ah, Mer…" Looking grim, he gulped the last of his wine down and, after putting down his glass, secured her against his body. "Do you think I'm happy about that?"

"No, of course not. But…why do you think he didn't come?"

"I don't know."

"I invited him as soon as you told me he wanted to be part of your life." Her expression turned doubtful. "Do you think he was just paying lip service to you about approving of me? Maybe he's decided I'm not good enough for you after all. Maybe his investigator turned up something about Mother that even I didn't know about."

Cain framed her face with his hands. "Stop. That's beyond nuts. Besides, anything your mother did has no reflection on you. And let me remind you that all indications are that he liked you before I even got out of prison. I'm as disappointed in him as I am offended for you."

"Do you think something could have happened?"

"You mean like an accident?" He shrugged. "He

gave me his business card to keep in touch with him if anything happened. Surely he knows that's supposed to work both ways."

"But you didn't have a phone number at the time."

"He has employees who know where to find me." Cain swore under his breath and began to turn away. "I'm going straight to him tomorrow and demand to know what made him think he could do this to you."

Merritt tightened her arms. "Oh, no, don't. If he fired you, I'd never forgive myself. Just…let it be. Maybe he'll explain in due time. You deserve this opportunity, Cain. Please take it."

For an endless moment, he looked like he was going to argue, but finally relented. "Speaking of opportunities…you should have seen your face when Alvie made her announcement."

"If my eyes bugged and my mouth hung open, that was just a start to my shock. As I said, I knew she wanted me to take on the business someday. But I thought we could work out some sort of payment plan, then pay her rent." She gestured helplessly. "Who gives away a life's work?"

"Someone who has found something they thought they'd lost forever or would never have." Cain folded her into his arms again. "And hopefully she's on the way to becoming the mother you should have had."

"She's the other blessing in my life, that's for sure." Merritt allowed herself a moment to dream. "I do have tons of ideas for the place and the business."

"It'll be lots of work."

"Since when did that ever intimidate me?"

Cain rested his forehead against hers. "Never, but

I'll worry that you're overdoing things. I've heard you whimper in your sleep from your hip hurting you, Merritt."

She'd hoped he was asleep. She'd woken a few times from hearing that herself. "Wait until the weather warms. You'll barely see me limp. And maybe in a year or so, if I can keep business growing as it is, I can save enough to pay for the surgery."

Sighing, Cain kissed her, then brushed his thumb over her lower lip. "Do you know what I don't want to wait to see?"

"What?"

"You in those earrings…and nothing else."

With a smile, Merritt took his hand. "Follow me."

When Cain made it to the ranch the next day, he started for the barn where he knew everyone was congregating given the vehicles already parked there. Despite Merritt's renewed plea this morning that he do nothing rash, he knew he had to talk to Sanford first. So he did a sharp about-face and headed for the house with determined strides. There he used the brass door knocker to announce his presence.

It took a good while, he had to knock again, but finally the door opened and Sanford stood before him looking more his age but dressed, as usual, like a gentleman cowboy in pressed jeans, a cashmere-wool Western-cut shirt in a soft camel and a darker tan leather vest.

"Somehow I thought it might be you," he said, stepping aside. "Come in."

"I'm due to ride out with the others. I can say what I need to say here, if you'd prefer."

"I don't. I'm cold and I need to sit down." Already walking away, Sanford motioned for him to follow. "Indulge me. Please."

He wasn't being impolite, just brief, Cain realized, seeing something in his stride that also hinted there would be an explanation. Closing the door, he followed him into his study. Even though he knew he'd done nothing wrong, he still felt as though he was being led to the warden's office. The house did lend to that atmosphere with its long logs and walls of stone. Cain eyed the wild game heads and thought of Merritt's reaction to them. She would admire the art though, and the furnishings that were sculpture in their own right.

In his office, Sanford stopped at a side table bearing a silver tray with an insulated coffeepot and four mugs. It was reassuring to see that they weren't fine china cups and saucers. On the other hand, they were sturdy and unusually shaped pieces of pottery, suggesting that they were one of a kind.

"Can I offer you some?" Sanford asked.

"No, thanks. I really shouldn't take any more of your time. Besides, they'll be wondering where I am."

"I saw Floyd spot you heading to the house. They'll wait on you." After pouring his coffee, Sanford asked, "How's Merritt?"

"Disappointed." He watched his grandfather sigh heavily then ease into the chair behind his desk. It was a rich black leather, and the desk was marble and mahogany. Cain thought it might as well be an ocean liner between them for the vast differences between the old man and himself.

"I'll bet you warned her that I wouldn't come?"

"I did."

"You were wrong. I was nervous, probably no less so than you were coming here, but I wanted to. Then I became ill while I was in Helena trying to do some last-minute Christmas shopping. I spent Christmas Eve night in the hospital. I only returned home at dusk last night."

Cain could see now that his coloring wasn't good and that even lifting the mug seemed to take an effort. "Why didn't you send some word?"

"Why ruin your Christmas?"

"Is there something I can do now?"

"Learn fast."

"Pardon?"

Sanford tapped his chest with his right index finger. "Hardware problem. I have to slow down. My doctor says if I don't, I won't see another Christmas. Crap timing. I was ready to clock out when I lost your grandmother, and then again when your father died. Particularly when Tom died. And now, for the first time in a long time, I actually enjoy opening my eyes in the morning and look what happens."

So Merritt's hunch about him being unwell was right. Cain had believed in the image of the man and his anger too well. So much that he hadn't believed illness could touch him.

"In that case," he told his grandfather with mild reproach, "don't you think you should lay off the caffeine?"

Sanford looked at the mug as though just realizing what he'd been doing. Then he muttered, "Well, this is going to be fun," and pushed it farther out of reach.

For the first time, Cain felt a touch of amusement. Somehow the playing field had been leveled and they were no longer power mogul and unwanted bastard. They were two men with shared blood and numerous disappointments littering their mutual landscape. Two men who had found something to believe in again. Cain figured he could deal with the old man from that perspective.

"There are things I want to know about you," Sanford said, as though picking up where Cain's thoughts left off. "If you'll allow me. There are also things you need to learn about running a ranch. I pray for both of our sakes that there's time for me to teach you."

While Cain knew the wisdom in that, he was still adjusting to the idea of being the "chosen one" after all. "Just like that?"

Sanford met his unwavering study with equal aplomb. "I understand your ingrained suspiciousness and the deserved impulse to spit in my face, but let's be honest, are you weighing another offer even remotely as tempting?"

Despite his caution and long-held resentment, Cain had the ability to see the question as a man, not a wounded boy. "Not today."

"No, and not tomorrow, either." Sanford began to reach for a wood and pewter box on the right corner of the blotter, then checked himself. "I'm not deluding myself into believing I can ever fix all that is damaged between us, but I can damn sure help you not lose this place even before I'm cold in the ground. Don't think that's self-pity talking, either. I'm hoping to last long enough to hold at least one great-grandchild in my arms."

Cain eyed the box that undoubtedly contained expensive cigars. "You better follow doctor's orders then, since I'm not even married yet."

"But you're in love. Don't insult my intelligence or vision and pretend otherwise. Marry that girl."

Cain remained silent.

"Fine," Sanford continued. "Be stubborn. I'll say my piece. I want to help her walk down the aisle as she was meant to walk."

It was easy to remain aloof himself, or just quietly grateful for a promise of change that allowed him to hope he could give Merritt the life she deserved. But to hear that she could be healed? Cain felt a pressure in his chest that threatened to choke him. Then, amazingly, he felt it lift and pass from him.

He breathed without resistance for the first time in... he didn't know how long.

"Now I know you're serious," he said quietly.

"Thank you."

"She's on your side, you know," Cain added. "She could see changes in you that I couldn't early on."

"Wouldn't."

"That, too."

Grunting, Sanford crossed one leg over the other and acknowledged the impulse of rejection with a wave of his hand. "I know this won't be easy. We'll fight. That's all right. Your father and I fought. A good argument is healthy. A heated debate keeps the mind agile. But never question this agreement between us, or doubt I mean what I'm doing."

Cain inclined his head. "We'll see."

With a short bark of laughter, Sanford slapped the blotter. "You are a Paxton." He reached into his desk drawer and brought out a box and set it within Cain's reach. "Hopefully, this will help Merritt believe my deep regret for disappointing her yesterday. It was your grandmother's. I would take it as a great gesture to her memory to see Merritt wear it."

He thought that the day outside the recruitment office had been an earth-shaking day. Cain eyed the box with a thudding heart. Slowly, he took the necessary step closer and picked it up, then lifted the lid. For several long seconds, he stared at it. Finally, he shut it and tucked it in his jacket pocket.

"I'll see what I can do."

On New Year's Eve, Merritt came home after changing her mind. At first, she'd thought it might be fun to have a paint party at the café—or rather the store next door that they were, indeed, going to adjoin to the rest of the restaurant. But it had been a busy few days and she agreed with Cain. Staying home and spending the time alone was the better idea. They hadn't seen that much of each other in the last few days. He'd been working long hours himself. But he seemed in good spirits and had told her that he liked the work and the people. He was even finding positive things to say about his grandfather when they weren't butting heads over one thing or another.

When she pulled into the driveway, Merritt had a

moment's pause when she didn't see the familiar, dirty and scratched black truck parked by the back stairs. In its place was a shiny silver one gleaming under the growing moon. That wasn't Josh Bevans's truck, she mused to herself, and it hadn't been but a year or two old. It would seem that Sanford had finally won a round of willpower with Cain.

Prepared to tease him royally, she opened the door to find him standing in candlelight over the kitchen table. A crystal vase holding a dozen red roses stood between the candles they'd last used at Christmas. Next to two of the holiday goblets was a bottle of champagne. She thought the pizza box was very much a Cain touch.

As he quickly shut the lid on the pizza, she guessed he'd been tempted to sneak a bite. "Getting impatient?"

"A little bit. I thought you'd like a chance not to have to cook for a change."

She grinned. "It's wonderful. And romantic. And you." She went directly to him and kissed him once for hello, once for missing him and once for being so dear and always thinking of her.

"I was going to tease you about the truck outside," she said, returning to the door to quickly get rid of her coat and boots. "But how can I after seeing how much effort you've put into tonight? What happened? Did Sanford have one of the guys intentionally drop a box of horseshoe nails behind your old truck's tires?" She knew his grandfather complained about the unsightly thing daily. However, that had just made Cain all the more determined to keep it running.

"Not quite. Transmission problems undermined me. Sanford grinned all the way to the dealership."

Merritt chuckled, too, finding it easy to visualize the trip and salty repartee the men had undoubtedly shared. She was glad that Sanford was following doctor's orders and feeling better. "It's a pretty flashy piece of machinery, Mr. Paxton."

"Yeah." He sighed, opening the champagne. "Damn it."

They both laughed and then there was the pop of the cork. Cain quickly poured the foaming wine.

When Merritt accepted one of the glasses, she touched it to his. "Happy New Year," she murmured.

"Happy New Year."

After a sip, Merritt motioned to the pizza. "Go ahead and dig in. I thought I'd change out of these work clothes. A child spilled a bowl of spaghetti and sauce on me and these jeans are trying to set like plaster."

"Go ahead. I'll wait."

"No really, you must be starving being in the fresh air all day." She set down her glass and started for the bedroom.

"It wouldn't be the same."

Merritt stopped, touched. "You never fail to say the dearest thing." She returned to pull out one chair and directed, "Sit." When he did, she settled on his lap then reached for the box. "How about we share the first slice, Mr. Romantic?"

As soon as she opened the lid, she gaped at the black satin box sitting on a little pad of foil to keep it clean. It was a very little box, not one to get confused with earrings or anything else.

"Oh, my God," she whispered, immediately clasping her hands in her lap.

"You can't be surprised." Cain opened it for her.

"Oh, my!"

The diamond engagement and wedding rings were clearly old and beyond beautiful. The engagement primary stone was square-cut and framed by four smaller diamonds on each side. The wedding band had six more diamonds. Both were set on platinum bands.

Taking the engagement ring out of the box, Cain said, "This was my grandmother's. My mother never got to wear it. I know she—and I'm sure my grandmother—would love for you to. Marry me, Mer. Be my first and last love."

"Yes," she breathed.

Taking a deep breath, she gave him her left hand. And for the first time that either of them could recall, her fingers were steady.

Once Cain slipped the ring on, she turned to kiss him. Her heart and soul was in that kiss.

"That was unbelievably generous of your grandfather," she said against his shoulder.

"You might want to call him. I've carried this with me since the day after Christmas. I told him that I'd choose my time and he would just have to deal with it. He's been a bear all week."

"I'll call him now," she began. But as she began to ease off of his lap, he stopped her.

"There's one more thing. He wants you to be able to walk without pain at our wedding."

Merritt closed her eyes, but there was no stopping the tears that seeped from beneath her lashes.

Cain kissed them away. "I know, darling. It's all good."

"No one deserves to be this happy."

"I think we all agree that you do."

She laid her hand against his beloved face. "It's really going to be all right, isn't it?" she asked him. "Finally, all right."

"Yes, my heart."

Epilogue

Valentine's Day

"I can't tell you how honored I am that you're allowing me to do this."

Sanford Paxton smiled tenderly at Merritt as the electric stair chair came to a gliding halt at the base of the Paxton house staircase. Merritt accepted his hand and rose from the seat. He had the chair installed because she'd told him that the timing wasn't right for her to undergo surgery at this time. Since his doctors had recommended he think of a bedroom on the main floor if he refused to have live-in help, Sanford assured Merritt it was for him, too.

"We're the blessed ones," she told him, rising on tiptoe to kiss his cheek. "For all you've done and for coming into our lives."

He blinked hard and stepped back to admire her. "You look like an angel."

For the first time, Merritt believed it. The white-lace, floor-length gown, with its narrow shirt and long sleeves, was ultrafeminine and flattered her slender shape. Her dark hair was brushed to a glow and tied over her left shoulder by matching lace enhanced by a white rose. Her diamond stud earrings and the garnet and diamond heart were the "something new" from Sanford and Cain—a Valentine's surprise—and her "something old" was the small white Bible Alvie lent her. It had been a gift to her child at her christening, and wrapped around it with white and red ribbon was the daintiest bouquet of red and white tea roses.

Life was good and getting better. Cain was enjoying his work at the ranch and growing to be more comfortable around his grandfather. They'd hit a bump or two over the last two months, but it was mostly out of Sanford's enthusiasm to help with their plans for the future. He had again tried to convince them to move to the ranch, but after discussing it, Cain told him that he wanted Merritt to have an easier commute to the café for now.

"Thank you," Merritt said, stroking his hand. She thought he looked dashing in his gray evening suit. "How are you feeling?"

"Ready for champagne." Sanford winked at her.

She knew he was teasing her. He had followed the specialists' advice to the nth degree regarding his health. That was proof that he treasured this new lease on life and wanted to share in every minute he was given.

"Let's get this done," he added, offering his arm.

Merritt pulled him back gently. "There's something I wanted to say first. Something you need to know. I told Cain I wanted to wait until this moment to put your mind at rest. The reason I'm delaying the operation? It isn't work. Just before I was due to have the surgery, I discovered I was pregnant. I felt, *we* felt, it was much safer for the baby that we wait until afterward."

"Pregnant." Sanford embraced her as gently as if she was spun glass. "Oh, darling girl. When?"

"Late August."

"I can't wait. I'm so pleased."

Kissing her cheek, he led her proudly to the parlor. As soon as the door opened, the music began, played by one of the hands—a fiddle player. Merritt looked immediately through the small gathering of perhaps twenty people—Alvie and Leroy and mostly the hands at the ranch with their spouses—and locked gazes with Cain.

She reached out to clasp Alvie's hand on the walk up. Then at the end of the short distance, Sanford gave her hand to Cain.

"I can't tell you how happy and grateful I am for you both. Congratulations."

As she and Cain squeezed each other's hands, they smiled. Merritt thought he looked nothing short of captivating in his new charcoal-gray suit and silver-and-gold-striped tie. His gaze made it clear that he couldn't take his eyes off of her. But as someone cleared their throat impatiently, they grinned and faced the minister.

Pastor Brannigan was from Alvie and Leroy's church.

The slight, elderly man nodded in welcome and approval and began, "Dearly beloved…"

As Merritt and Cain gazed peacefully into each other's eyes, they jointly said, "Yes."

Minutes later it was done. Even before Cain could kiss his bride, the ranch hands were whistling and the other guests were clapping. Merritt saw Alvie dabbing at her eyes and Leroy hugging her against him.

"Mrs. Paxton," Cain murmured against her lips.

It was the perfect Valentine's Day. The first time she'd given the holiday more than a thought. They accepted congratulations and hugs, and made their way to the cake and champagne. Sanford had wanted to throw a big catered party followed by an extravagant honeymoon, but she and Cain had wanted to keep things as low-key as possible. This was just the formality of what was already in their hearts.

Their idea of a perfect honeymoon was going to be the weekend alone at the cottage with no alarm clocks forcing them out of bed before dawn and no deadlines or chores unless they wanted to do them. This was their time to linger over meals they would make together and to celebrate their love.

Sanford had been dejected at first. Now, as they cut the two-tiered heart-shaped cake with the red roses, his expression was serene, his understanding complete.

As Merritt watched Cain lick icing off of her finger, she must have had a knowing twinkle in her eye because he leaned close to her ear and asked, "Are you thinking what I'm thinking?"

"Escape and spend the rest of the day just the two of us?"

"Just the three of us," he amended, sneaking a soft kiss below her ear while he brushed her stomach.

"Let's do it."

And as they made way for Alvie to take over portioning out cake and Leroy called everyone over as he poured champagne, the circle around the table closed, allowing Merritt and Cain to slip out the front door— and into their lives together.

* * * * *

A sneaky peek at next month...

Cherish™

ROMANCE TO MELT THE HEART EVERY TIME

My wish list for next month's titles...

In stores from 20th April 2012:

❑ The Cop, the Puppy and Me – Cara Colter

& Courtney's Baby Plan – Allison Leigh

❑ Daddy on Her Doorstep – Lilian Darcy

& Courting His Favourite Nurse – Lynne Marshall

In stores from 4th May 2012:

❑ The Cattle King's Bride – Margaret Way

& The Last Real Cowboy – Donna Alward

❑ Taming the Lost Prince – Raye Morgan

& Inherited: Expectant Cinderella – Myrna Mackenzie

Available at WHSmith, Tesco, Asda, Eason, Amazon and Apple

Just can't wait?

 **Special Offers**

Every month we put together collections and longer reads written by your favourite authors.

Here are some of next month's highlights— and don't miss our fabulous discount online!

On sale 20th April

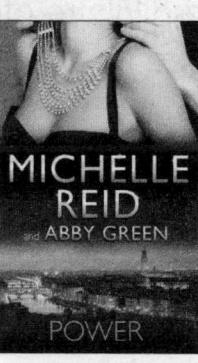

On sale 20th April

On sale 20th April

The World of Mills & Boon®

There's a Mills & Boon® series that's perfect for you. We publish ten series and with new titles every month, you never have to wait long for your favourite to come along.

Blaze.
Scorching hot, sexy reads

By Request
Relive the romance with the best of the best

Cherish
Romance to melt the heart every time

Desire
Passionate and dramatic love stories

Have Your Say

*You've just finished your book.
So what did you think?*

We'd love to hear your thoughts on our
'Have your say' online panel
www.millsandboon.co.uk/haveyoursay

- Easy to use
- Short questionnaire
- Chance to win Mills & Boon® goodies